A Dance of Folly and Pleasure

A Dance of Folly and Pleasure

Stories

O. HENRY

DAUNT BOOKS

This edition first published in 2012 by
Daunt Books
83 Marylebone High Street
London W1U 4QW

1

A CIP catalogue record for this title is available
from the British Library.

ISBN 978 1 907970 10 8

Typeset by Antony Gray
Printed and bound by
TJ International Ltd, Padstow, Cornwall

www.dauntbooks.co.uk

Contents

The Gift of the Magi

One dollar and eighty-seven cents. That was all. And sixty cents of it was in pennies. Pennies saved one and two at a time by bulldozing the grocer and the vegetable man and the butcher until one's cheek burned with the silent imputation of parsimony that such close dealing implied. Three times Della counted it. One dollar and eighty-seven cents. And the next day would be Christmas.

There was clearly nothing left to do but flop down on the shabby little couch and howl. So Della did it. Which instigates the moral reflection that life is made up of sobs, sniffles and smiles, with sniffles predominating.

While the mistress of the home is gradually subsiding from the first stage to the second, take a look at the home. A furnished flat at eight dollars per week. It did not exactly beggar description, but it certainly had that word on the look-out for the mendicancy squad.

In the vestibule below was a letter box into which no letter would go, and an electric button from which no mortal finger could coax a ring. Also appertaining thereunto was a card bearing the name 'Mr James Dillingham Young'.

The 'Dillingham' had been flung to the breeze during a former period of prosperity when its possessor was being paid thirty dollars per week. Now, when the income was shrunk to twenty dollars, the letters of 'Dillingham' looked blurred, as though they were thinking seriously of contracting to a modest and unassuming D. But whenever Mr James Dillingham

Young came home and reached his flat above he was called 'Jim' and greatly hugged by Mrs James Dillingham Young, already introduced to you as Della. Which is all very good.

Della finished her cry and attended to her cheeks with the powder rag. She stood by the window and looked out dully at a grey cat walking a grey fence in a grey backyard. Tomorrow would be Christmas Day, and she had only one dollar and eighty-seven cents with which to buy Jim a present. She had been saving every penny she could for months, with this result. Twenty dollars a week doesn't go far. Expenses had been greater than she had calculated. They always are. Only one dollar and eighty-seven cents to buy a present for Jim. Her Jim. Many a happy hour she had spent planning for something nice for him. Something fine and rare and sterling – something just a little bit near to being worthy of the honour of being owned by Jim.

There was a pier-glass between the windows of the room. Perhaps you have seen a pier-glass in an eight dollar flat. A very thin and very agile person may, by observing his reflection in a rapid sequence of longitudinal strips, obtain a fairly accurate conception of his looks. Della, being slender, had mastered the art.

Suddenly she whirled from the window and stood before the glass. Her eyes were shining brilliantly, but her face had lost its colour within twenty seconds. Rapidly she pulled down her hair and let it fall to its full length.

Now, there were two possessions of the James Dillingham Youngs in which they both took a mighty pride. One was Jim's gold watch that had been his father's and his grand-father's. The other was Della's hair. Had the Queen of Sheba lived in the flat across the air shaft, Della would have let her hair hang out the window some day to dry just to depreciate

Her Majesty's jewels and gifts. Had King Solomon been the janitor, with all his treasures piled up in the basement, Jim would have pulled out his watch every time he passed, just to see him pluck at his beard from envy.

So now Della's beautiful hair fell about her, rippling and shining like a cascade of brown waters. It reached below her knee and made itself almost a garment for her. And then she did it up again nervously and quickly. Once she faltered for a minute and stood still while a tear or two splashed on the worn red carpet.

On went her old brown jacket; on went her old brown hat. With a whirl of skirts and with the brilliant sparkle still in her eyes, she fluttered out of the door and down the stairs to the street.

Where she stopped the sign read: 'Mme Sofronie. Hair Goods of All Kinds.' One flight up Della ran, and collected herself, panting. Madame, large, too white, chilly, hardly looked the 'Sofronie'.

'Will you buy my hair?' asked Della.

'I buy hair,' said Madame. 'Take yer hat off and let's have a sight at the looks of it.'

Down rippled the brown cascade.

'Twenty dollars,' said Madame, lifting the mass with a practised hand.

'Give it to me quick,' said Della.

Oh, and the next two hours tripped by on rosy wings. Forget the hashed metaphor. She was ransacking the stores for Jim's present.

She found it at last. It surely had been made for Jim and no one else. There was no other like it in any of the stores, and she had turned all of them inside out. It was a platinum fob chain simple and chaste in design, properly proclaiming its value by substance alone and not by meretricious ornamentation – as all good things should do. It was even worthy of The Watch. As soon as she saw it she knew that it must be Jim's. It was like him. Quietness and value – the description applied to both. Twenty-one dollars they took from her for it, and she hurried home with the eighty-seven cents. With that chain on his watch, Jim might be properly anxious about the time in any company. Grand as the watch was, he sometimes looked at it on the sly on account of the old leather strap that he used in place of a chain.

When Della reached home her intoxication gave way a little to prudence and reason. She got out her curling irons and lighted the gas and went to work repairing the ravages made by generosity added to love. Which is always a tremendous task, dear friends – a mammoth task.

Within forty minutes her head was covered with tiny, close-lying curls that made her look wonderfully like a truant school-boy. She looked at her reflection in the mirror long, carefully and critically.

'If Jim doesn't kill me,' she said to herself, 'before he takes a second look at me, he'll say I look like a Coney Island chorus girl. But what could I do – oh! what could I do with a dollar and eighty-seven cents?'

At seven o'clock the coffee was made and the frying-pan was on the back of the stove, hot and ready to cook the chops.

Jim was never late. Della doubled the fob chain in her hand and sat on the corner of the table near the door that he always entered. Then she heard his step on the stair away down on the first flight, and she turned white for just a moment. She had a habit of saying little silent prayers about the simplest everyday things, and now she whispered: 'Please God, make him think I am still pretty.'

The door opened and Jim stepped in and closed it. He

looked thin and very serious. Poor fellow, he was only twenty-two – and to be burdened with a family! He needed a new overcoat and he was without gloves.

Jim stepped inside the door, as immovable as a setter at the scent of quail. His eyes were fixed upon Della, and there was an expression in them that she could not read, and it terrified her. It was not anger, nor surprise, nor disapproval, nor horror, nor any of the sentiments that she had been prepared for. He simply stared at her fixedly with that peculiar expression on his face.

Della wriggled off the table and went for him.

'Jim, darling,' she cried, 'don't look at me that way. I had my hair cut off and sold it because I couldn't have lived through Christmas without giving you a present. It'll grow out again – you won't mind, will you? I just had to do it. My hair grows awfully fast. Say "Merry Christmas!" Jim, and let's be happy. You don't know what a nice – what a beautiful, nice gift I've got for you.'

'You've cut off your hair?' asked Jim, laboriously, as if he had not arrived at that patent fact yet even after the hardest mental labour.

'Cut it off and sold it,' said Della. 'Don't you like me just as well, anyhow? I'm me without my hair, ain't I?'

Jim looked about the room curiously.

'You say your hair is gone?' he said with an air almost of idiocy.

'You needn't look for it,' said Della. 'It's sold, I tell you – sold and gone, too. It's Christmas Eve, boy. Be good to me, for it went for you. Maybe the hairs of my head were numbered,' she went on with a sudden serious sweetness, 'but nobody could ever count my love for you. Shall I put the chops on, Jim?'

Out of his trance Jim seemed quickly to wake. He enfolded his Della. For ten seconds let us regard with discreet scrutiny some inconsequential object in the other direction. Eight dollars a week or a million a year – what is the difference? A mathematician or a wit would give you the wrong answer. The magi brought valuable gifts, but that was not among them. This dark assertion will be illuminated later on.

Jim drew a package from his overcoat pocket and threw it upon the table.

'Don't make any mistake, Dell,' he said, 'about me. I don't think there's anything in the way of a haircut or a shave or a shampoo that could make me like my girl any less. But if you'll unwrap that package you may see why you had me going awhile at first.'

White fingers and nimble tore at the string and paper. And then an ecstatic scream of joy; and then, alas! a quick feminine change to hysterical tears and wails, necessitating the immediate employment of all the comforting powers of the lord of the flat.

For there lay The Combs – the set of combs, side and back, that Della had worshipped for long in a Broadway window. Beautiful combs, pure tortoiseshell, with jewelled rims – just the shade to wear in the beautiful vanished hair. They were expensive combs, she knew, and her heart had simply craved and yearned over them without the least hope of possession. And now they were hers, but the tresses that should have adorned the coveted adornments were gone.

But she hugged them to her bosom, and at length she was able to look up with dim eyes and a smile and say: 'My hair grows so fast, Jim!'

And then Della leaped up like a little singed cat and cried, 'Oh, oh!'

Jim had not yet seen his beautiful present. She held it out to him eagerly upon her open palm. The dull precious metal seemed to flash with a reflection of her bright and ardent spirit.

'Isn't it a dandy, Jim? I hunted all over town to find it. You'll have to look at the time a hundred times a day now. Give me your watch. I want to see how it looks on it.'

Instead of obeying, Jim tumbled down on the couch and put his hands under the back of his head and smiled.

'Dell,' said he, 'let's put our Christmas presents away and keep 'em awhile. They're too nice to use just at present. I sold the watch to get the money to buy your combs. And now suppose you put the chops on.'

The magi, as you know, were wise men – wonderfully wise men – who brought gifts to the Babe in the manger. They invented the art of giving Christmas presents. Being wise, their gifts were no doubt wise ones, possibly bearing the privilege of exchange in case of duplication. And here I have lamely related to you the uneventful chronicle of two foolish children in a flat who most unwisely sacrificed for each other the greatest treasures of their house. But in a last word to the wise of these days, let it be said that of all who give gifts these two were the wisest. Of all who give and receive gifts, such as they are wisest. Everywhere they are wisest. They are the magi.

The Cop and the Anthem

On his bench in Madison Square, Soapy moved uneasily. When wild goose honk high of nights, and when women without sealskin coats grow kind to their husbands, and when Soapy moves uneasily on his bench in the park, you may know that winter is near at hand.

A dead leaf fell in Soapy's lap. That was Jack Frost's card. Jack is kind to the regular denizens of Madison Square, and gives fair warning of his annual call. At the corners of four streets he hands his pasteboard to the North Wind, footman of the mansion of All Outdoors, so that the inhabitants thereof may make ready.

Soapy's mind became cognisant of the fact that the time had come for him to resolve himself into a singular Committee of Ways and Means to provide against the coming rigour. And therefore he moved uneasily his bench.

The hibernatorial ambitions of Soapy were not of the highest. In them were no considerations of Mediterranean cruises, of soporific Southern skies or drifting in the Vesuvian Bay. Three months on the Island was what his soul craved. Three months of assured board and bed and congenial company, safe from Boreas and blue coats, seemed to Soapy the essence of things desirable.

For years the hospitable Blackwell's had been his winter quarters. Just as his more fortunate fellow New Yorkers had bought their tickets to Palm Beach and the Riviera each winter, so Soapy had made his humble arrangements for his annual Hegira to the Island. And now the time was come. On the previous night three Sabbath newspapers, distributed beneath his coat, about his ankles and over his lap, had failed to repulse the cold as he slept on his bench near the spurting fountain in the ancient square. So the Island loomed large and timely in Soapy's mind. He scorned the provisions made in the name of charity for the city's dependents. In Soapy's opinion the Law was more benign than Philanthropy. There was an endless round of institutions, municipal and eleemosynary, on which he might set out and receive lodging and food accordant with the simple life. But to one of Soapy's proud spirit the gifts of charity are encumbered. If not in coin you must pay in humiliation of spirit for every benefit received at the hands of philanthropy. As Caesar had his Brutus, every bed of charity must have its toll of a bath, every loaf of bread its compensation of a private and personal inquisition. Wherefore it is better to be a guest of the law, which, though conducted by rules, does not meddle unduly with a gentleman's private affairs

Soapy, having decided to go to the Island, at once set about accomplishing his desire. There were many easy ways of doing this. The pleasantest was to dine luxuriously at some expensive restaurant; and then, after declaring insolvency, be handed over quietly and without uproar to a policeman. An accommodating magistrate would do the rest.

Soapy left his bench and strolled out of the square and across the level sea of asphalt, where Broadway and Fifth Avenue flow together. Up Broadway he turned, and halted at a glittering café, where are gathered together nightly the choicest products of the grape, the silkworm and the protoplasm.

Soapy had confidence in himself from the lowest button of

his vest upward. He was shaven, and his coat was decent and his neat black, ready-tied four-in-hand had been presented to him by a lady missionary on Thanksgiving Day. If he could reach a table in the restaurant unsuspected success would be his. The portion of him that would show above the table would raise no doubt in the waiter's mind. A roasted mallard duck, thought Soapy, would be about the thing – with a bottle of Chablis, and then Camembert, a demi-tasse and a cigar. One dollar for the cigar would be enough. The total would not be so high as to call forth any supreme manifestation of revenge from the café management; and yet the meat would leave him filled and happy for the journey to his winter refuge.

But as Soapy set foot inside the restaurant door the head waiter's eye fell upon his frayed trousers and decadent shoes. Strong and ready hands turned him about and conveyed him in silence and haste to the sidewalk and averted the ignoble fate of the menaced mallard.

Soapy turned off Broadway. It seemed that his route to the coveted Island was not to be an epicurean one. Some other way of entering limbo must be thought of.

At a corner of Sixth Avenue electric lights and cunningly displayed wares behind plate-glass made a shop window conspicuous. Soapy took a cobblestone and dashed it through the glass. People came running round the corner, a policeman in the lead. Soapy stood still, with his hands in his pockets, and smiled at the sight of brass buttons.

'Where's the man that done that?' enquired the officer excitedly.

'Don't you figure out that I might have had something to do with it?' said Soapy, not without sarcasm, but friendly, as one greets good fortune.

The policeman's mind refused to accept Soapy even as a

clue. Men who smash windows do not remain to parley with the law's minions. They take to their heels. The policeman saw a man halfway down the block running to catch a car. With drawn club he joined in the pursuit. Soapy, with disgust in his heart, loafed along, twice unsuccessful.

On the opposite side of the street was a restaurant of no great pretensions. It catered to large appetites and modest purses. Its crockery and atmosphere were thick; its soup and napery thin. Into this place Soapy took his accusive shoes and telltale trousers without challenge. At a table he sat and consumed beef steak, pancakes, doughnuts and pie. And then to the waiter he betrayed the fact that the minutest coin and himself were strangers.

'Now, get busy and call a cop,' said Soapy. 'And don't keep a gentleman waiting.'

'No cop for youse,' said the waiter, with a voice like butter cakes and an eye like the cherry in a Manhattan cocktail. 'Hey, Con!'

Neatly upon his left ear on the callous pavement two waiters pitched Soapy. He arose, joint by joint, as a carpenter's rule opens, and beat the dust from his clothes. Arrest seemed but a rosy dream. The Island seemed very far away. A policeman who stood before a drugstore two doors away laughed and walked down the street.

Five blocks Soapy travelled before his courage permitted him to woo capture again. This time the opportunity presented what he fatuously termed to himself a 'cinch'. A young woman of a modest and pleasing guise was standing before a show window gazing with sprightly interest at its display of shaving mugs and inkstands, and two yards from the window a large policeman of severe demeanour leaned against a water-plug.

It was Soapy's design to assume the role of the despicable and execrated 'masher'. The refined and elegant appearance of his victim and the contiguity of the conscientious cop encouraged him to believe that he would soon feel the pleasant official clutch upon his arm that would ensure his winter quarters on the right little, tight little isle.

Soapy straightened the lady missionary's ready-made tie, dragged his shrinking cuffs into the open, set his hat at a killing cant and sidled toward the young woman. He made eyes at her, was taken with sudden coughs and 'hems', smiled, smirked and went brazenly through the impudent and contemptible litany of the 'masher'. With half an eye Soapy saw that the policeman was watching him fixedly. The young woman moved away a few steps, and again bestowed her absorbed attention upon the shaving mugs. Soapy followed, boldly stepping to her side, raised his hat and said: 'Ah there, Bedelia! Don't you want to come and play in my yard?'

The policeman was still looking. The persecuted young woman had but to beckon a finger and Soapy would be practically *en route* for his insular haven. Already he imagined he could feel the cosy warmth of the station-house. The young woman faced him and, stretching out a hand, caught Soapy's coat-sleeve.

'Sure, Mike,' she said joyfully, 'if you'll blow me to a pail of suds. I'd have spoke to you sooner, but the cop was watching.'

With the young woman playing the clinging ivy to his oak Soapy walked past the policeman, overcome with gloom. He seemed doomed to liberty.

At the next corner he shook off his companion and ran. He halted in the district where by night are found the lightest streets, hearts, vows and librettos. Women in furs and men in greatcoats moved gaily in the wintry air. A sudden fear seized

Soapy that some dreadful enchantment had rendered him immune to arrest. The thought brought a little of panic upon it, and when he came upon another policeman lounging grandly in front of a transplendent theatre he caught at the immediate straw of 'disorderly conduct'.

On the sidewalk Soapy began to yell drunken gibberish at the top of his harsh voice. He danced, howled, raved and otherwise disturbed the welkin.

The policeman twirled his club, turned his back to Soapy and remarked to a citizen: ''Tis one of them Yale lads celebratin' the goose egg they give to the Hartford College. Noisy; but no harm. We've instructions to lave them be.'

Disconsolate, Soapy ceased his unavailing racket. Would never a policeman lay hands on him? In his fancy the Island seemed an unattainable Arcadia. He buttoned his thin coat against the chilling wind.

In a cigar store he saw a well-dressed man lighting a cigar at a swinging light. His silk umbrella he had set by the door on entering. Soapy stepped inside, secured the umbrella and sauntered off with it slowly. The man at the cigar light followed hastily.

'My umbrella,' he said sternly.

'Oh, is it?' sneered Soapy, adding insult to petit larceny. 'Well, why don't you call a policeman? I took it. Your umbrella! Why don't you call a cop? There stands one at the corner.'

The umbrella owner slowed his steps. Soapy did likewise, with a presentiment that luck would again run against him. The policeman looked at the two curiously.

'Of course,' said the umbrella man – 'that is – well, you know how these mistakes occur – I – if it's your umbrella I hope you'll excuse me – I picked it up this morning in a restaurant – If you recognise it as yours, why – I hope you'll—'

'Of course it's mine,' said Soapy viciously.

The ex-umbrella man retreated. The policeman hurried to assist a tall blonde in an opera cloak across the street in front of a street car that was approaching two blocks away.

Soapy walked eastward through a street damaged by improvements. He hurled the umbrella wrathfully into an excavation. He muttered against the men who wear helmets and carry clubs. Because he wanted to fall into their clutches, they seemed to regard him as a king who could do no wrong.

At length Soapy reached one of the avenues to the east where the glitter and turmoil was but faint. He set his face down this toward Madison Square, for the homing instinct survives even when the home is a park bench.

But on an unusually quiet corner Soapy came to a standstill. Here was an old church, quaint and rambling and gabled. Through one violet-stained window a soft light glowed, where, no doubt, the organist loitered over the keys, making sure of his mastery of the coming Sabbath anthem. For there drifted out to Soapy's ears sweet music that caught and held him transfixed against the convolutions of the iron fence.

The moon was above, lustrous and serene; vehicles and pedestrians were few; sparrows twittered sleepily in the eaves – for a little while the scene might have been a country churchyard. And the anthem that the organist played cemented Soapy to the iron fence, for he had known it well in the days when his life contained such things as mothers and roses and ambitions and friends and immaculate thoughts and collars.

The conjunction of Soapy's receptive state of mind and the influences about the old church wrought a sudden and wonderful change in his soul. He viewed with swift horror the pit into which he had tumbled, the degraded days, unworthy desires, dead hopes, wrecked faculties and base motives that made up his existence.

And also in a moment his heart responded thrillingly to this novel mood. An instantaneous and strong impulse moved him to battle with his desperate fate. He would pull himself out of the mire; he would make a man of himself again; he would conquer the evil that had taken possession of him. There was time; he was comparatively young yet; he would resurrect his old eager ambitions and pursue them without faltering. Those solemn but sweet organ notes had set up a revolution in him. Tomorrow he would go into the roaring downtown district and find work. A fur importer had once offered him a place as driver. He would find him tomorrow and ask for the position. He would be somebody in the world. He would—

Soapy felt a hand laid on his arm. He looked quickly around into the broad face of a policeman.

'What are you doin' here?' asked the officer.

'Nothin',' said Soapy.

'Then come along,' said the policeman.

'Three months on the Island,' said the Magistrate in the Police Court the next morning.

The Love-Philtre of Ikey Schoenstein

The Blue Light Drugstore is downtown, between the Bowery and First Avenue, where the distance between the two streets is the shortest. The Blue Light does not consider that pharmacy is a thing of bric-à-brac, scent and ice-cream soda. If you ask it for a painkiller it will not give you a bonbon.

The Blue Light scorns the labour-saving arts of modern pharmacy. It macerates its opium and percolates its own laudanum and paregoric. To this day pills are made behind its tall prescription desk – pills rolled out on its own pill-tile, divided with a spatula, rolled with the finger and thumb, dusted with calcined magnesia and delivered in little round, pasteboard pill-boxes. The store is on a corner about which coveys of ragged-plumed, hilarious children play and become candidates for the cough-drops and soothing syrups that wait for them inside.

Ikey Schoenstein was the night clerk of the Blue Light and the friend of his customers. Thus it is on the East Side, where the heart of pharmacy is not *glacé*. There, as it should be, the druggist is a counsellor, a confessor, an adviser, an able and willing missionary and mentor whose learning is respected, whose occult wisdom is venerated and whose medicine is often poured, untasted, into the gutter. Therefore Ikey's corniform, bespectacled nose and narrow, knowledge-bowed figure was well known in the vicinity of the Blue Light, and his advice and notice were much desired.

Ikey roomed and breakfasted at Mrs Riddle's, two squares

away. Mrs Riddle had a daughter named Rosy. The circumlocution has been in vain – you must have guessed it – Ikey adored Rosy. She tinctured all his thoughts; she was the compound extract of all that was chemically pure and officinal – the dispensatory contained nothing equal to her. But Ikey was timid, and his hopes remained insoluble in the menstruum of his backwardness and fears. Behind his counter he was a superior being, calmly conscious of special knowledge and worth; outside, he was a weak-kneed, purblind, motorman-cursed rambler, with ill-fitting clothes stained with chemicals and smelling of socotrine aloes and valerianate of ammonia.

The fly in Ikey's ointment (thrice welcome, pat trope!) was Chunk McGowan.

Mr McGowan was also striving to catch the bright smiles tossed about by Rosy. But he was no outfielder as Ikey was; he picked them off the bat. At the same time he was Ikey's friend and customer, and often dropped in at the Blue Light Drugstore to have a bruise painted with iodine or get a cut rubber-plastered after a pleasant evening spent along the Bowery.

One afternoon McGowan drifted in in his silent, easy way, and sat, comely, smoothed-faced, hard, indomitable, good-natured, upon a stool.

'Ikey,' said he, when his friend had fetched his mortar and sat opposite, grinding gum benzoin to a powder, 'get busy with your ear. It's drugs for me if you've got the line I need.'

Ikey scanned the countenance of Mr McGowan for the usual evidences of conflict, but found none.

'Take your coat off,' he ordered. 'I guess already that you have been stuck in the ribs with a knife. I have many times told you those Dagoes would do you up.'

Mr McGowan smiled. 'Not them,' he said. 'Not any Dagoes. But you've located the diagnosis all right enough – it's under my coat, near the ribs. Say! Ikey – Rosy and me are goin' to run away and get married tonight.'

Ikey's left forefinger was doubled over the edge of the mortar, holding it steady. He gave it a wild rap with the pestle, but felt it not. Meanwhile Mr McGowan's smile faded to a look of perplexed gloom.

'That is,' he continued, 'if she keeps in the notion until the time comes. We've been layin' pipes for the gateway for two weeks. One day she says she will; the same evenin' she says nixy. We've agreed on tonight, and Rosy's stuck to the affirmative this time for two whole days. But it's five hours yet till the time, and I'm afraid she'll stand me up when it comes to the scratch.'

'You said you wanted drugs,' remarked Ikey.

Mr McGowan looked ill at ease and harassed – a condition opposed to his usual line of demeanour. He made a patent-medicine almanac into a roll and fitted it with unprofitable carefulness about his finger.

'I wouldn't have this double handicap make a false start tonight for a million,' he said. 'I've got a little flat up in Harlem all ready, with chrysanthemums on the table and a kettle ready to boil. And I've engaged a pulpit pounder to be ready at his house for us at 9.30. It's got to come off. And if Rosy don't change her mind again!' – Mr McGowan ceased, a prey to his doubts.

'I don't see then yet,' said Ikey shortly, 'what makes it that you talk of drugs, or what I can be doing about it.'

'Old man Riddle don't like me a little bit,' went on the uneasy suitor, bent upon marshalling his arguments. 'For a week he hasn't let Rosy step outside the door with me. If it wasn't for losin' a boarder they'd have bounced me long ago. I'm makin' twenty dollars a week and she'll never regret flyin' the coop with Chunk McGowan.'

'You will excuse me, Chunk,' said Ikey. 'I must make a prescription that is to be called for soon.'

'Say,' said McGowan, looking up suddenly, 'say, Ikey, ain't there a drug of some kind – some kind of powders that'll make a girl like you better if you give 'em to her?'

Ikey's lip beneath his nose curled with the scorn of superior enlightenment; but before he could answer, McGowan continued: 'Tim Lacy told me once that he got some from a croaker uptown and fed 'em to his girl in soda water. From the very first dose he was ace-high and everybody else looked like thirty cents to her. They was married in less than two weeks.'

Strong and simple was Chunk McGowan. A better reader of men than Ikey was could have seen that his tough frame was strung upon fine wires. Like a good general who was about to invade the enemy's territory he was seeking to guard every point against possible failure.

'I thought,' went on Chunk hopefully, 'that if I had one of them powders to give Rosy when I see her at supper tonight it might brace her up and keep her from reneging on the proposition to skip. I guess she don't need a mule team to drag her away, but women are better at coaching than they are at running bases. If the stuff'll work just for a couple of hours it'll do the trick.'

'When is this foolishness of running away to be happening?' asked Ikey.

'Nine o'clock,' said Mr McGowan. 'Supper's at seven. At eight Rosy goes to bed with a headache. At nine old Parvenzano lets me through to his backyard, where there's a board off Riddle's fence, next door. I go under her window and help her down the fire escape. We've got to make it early on the preacher's account. It's all dead easy if Rosy don't balk when the flag drops. Can you fix me one of them powders, Ikey?'

Ikey Schoenstein rubbed his nose slowly.

'Chunk,' said he, 'it is of drugs of that nature that pharmaceutists must have much carefulness. To you alone of my acquaintance would I entrust a powder like that. But for you I shall make it, and you shall see how it makes Rosy to think of you.'

Ikey went behind the prescription desk. There he crushed to a powder two soluble tablets, each containing a quarter of a grain of morphia. To them he added a little sugar of milk to increase the bulk, and folded the mixture neatly in a white paper. Taken by an adult this powder would ensure several hours of heavy slumber without danger to the sleeper. This he handed to Chunk McGowan, telling him to administer it in a liquid, if possible, and received the hearty thanks of the backyard Lochinvar.

The subtlety of Ikey's action becomes apparent upon recital of his subsequent move. He sent a messenger for Mr Riddle and disclosed the plans of McGowan for eloping with Rosy. Mr Riddle was a stout man, brick-dusty of complexion and sudden in action.

'Much obliged,' he said briefly to Ikey. 'The lazy Irish loafer! My own room's just above Rosy's. I'll just go up there myself after supper and load the shotgun and wait. If he comes in my backyard he'll go away in an ambulance instead of a bridal chaise.'

With Rosy held in the clutches of Morpheus for a many-hours' deep slumber, and the bloodthirsty parent waiting, armed and forewarned, Ikey felt that his rival was close, indeed, upon discomfiture.

All night in the Blue Light Store he waited at his duties for chance news of the tragedy, but none came.

At eight o'clock in the morning the day clerk arrived and Ikey started hurriedly for Mrs Riddle's to learn the outcome. And, lo! as he stepped out of the store who but Chunk McGowan sprang from a passing streetcar and grasped his hand – Chunk McGowan with a victor's smile and flushed with joy.

'Pulled it off,' said Chunk with Elysium in his grin. 'Rosy hit the fire escape on time to a second and we was under the wire at the Reverend's at 9.30. She's up at the flat – she cooked eggs this mornin' in a blue kimono – Lord! how lucky I am! You must pace up some day, Ikey, and feed with us. I've got a job down near the bridge, and that's where I'm heading for now.'

'The – the powder?' stammered Ikey.

'Oh, that stuff you gave me!' said Chunk broadening his grin; 'well, it was this way. I sat down at the supper table last night at Riddle's, and I looked at Rosy, and I says to myself, "Chunk, if you get the girl get her on the square – don't try any hocus-pocus with a thoroughbred like her." And I keeps the paper you give me in my pocket. And then my lamps falls on another party present, who, I says to myself, is failin' in a proper affection toward his comin' son-in-law, so I watches my chance and dumps that powder in old man Riddle's coffee – see?'

The Social Triangle

At the stroke of six Ikey Snigglefritz laid down his goose. Ikey was a tailor's apprentice. Are there tailor's apprentices nowadays?

At any rate, Ikey toiled and snipped and basted and pressed and patched and sponged all day in the steamy fetor of a tailor-shop. But when work was done Ikey hitched his wagon to such stars as his firmament let shine.

It was Saturday night, and the boss laid twelve begrimed and begrudged dollars in his hand. Ikey dabbled discreetly in water, donned coat, hat and collar with its frazzled tie and chalcedony pin, and set forth in pursuit of his ideals.

For each of us, when our day's work is done, must seek our ideal, whether it be love or pinochle or lobster à la Newburg, or the sweet silence of the musty bookshelves.

Behold Ikey as he ambles up the street beneath the roaring 'El' between the rows of reeking sweatshops. Pallid, stooping, insignificant, squalid, doomed to exist for ever in penury of body and mind, yet, as he swings his cheap cane and projects the noisome inhalations from his cigarette, you perceive that he nurtures in his narrow bosom the bacillus of society.

Ikey's legs carried him to and into that famous place of entertainment known as the Café Maginnis – famous because it was the rendezvous of Billy McMahan, the greatest man, the most wonderful man, Ikey thought, that the world had ever produced.

Billy McMahan was the district leader. Upon him the Tiger

purred, and his hand held manna to scatter. Now, as Ikey entered, McMahan stood, flushed and triumphant and mighty, the centre of a huzzaing concourse of his lieutenants and constituents. It seems there had been an election; a signal victory had been won; the city had been swept back into line by a resistless besom of ballots.

Ikey slunk along the bar and gazed, breath-quickened, at his idol.

How magnificent was Billy McMahan, with his great, smooth, laughing face; his grey eye, shrewd as a chicken hawk's; his diamond ring, his voice like a bugle call, his prince's air, his plump and active roll of money, his clarion call to friend and comrade – oh, what a king of men he was! How he obscured his lieutenants, though they themselves loomed large and serious, blue of chin and important of mien, with hands buried deep in the pockets of their short overcoats! But Billy – oh, what small avail are words to paint for you his glory as seen by Ikey Snigglefritz!

The Café Maginnis rang to the note of victory. The white-coated bartenders threw themselves featfully upon bottle, cork and glass. From a score of clear Havanas the air received its paradox of clouds. The leal and the hopeful shook Billy McMahan's hand. And there was born suddenly in the worshipful soul of Ikey Snigglefritz an audacious, thrilling impulse.

He stepped forward into the little cleared space in which majesty moved, and held out his hand.

Billy McMahan grasped it unhesitatingly, shook it and smiled.

Made mad now by the gods who were about to destroy him, Ikey threw away his scabbard and charged upon Olympus.

'Have a drink with me, Billy,' he said familiarly, 'you and your friends?'

'Don't mind if I do, old man,' said the great leader, 'just to keep the ball rolling.'

The last spark of Ikey's reason fled.

'Wine,' he called to the bartender, waving a trembling hand.

The corks of three bottles were drawn; the champagne bubbled in the long row of glasses set upon the bar. Billy McMahan took his and nodded, with his beaming smile, at Ikey. The lieutenants and satellites took theirs and growled 'Here's to you.' Ikey took his nectar in delirium. All drank.

Ikey threw his week's wages in a crumpled roll upon the bar.

'C'rect,' said the bartender, smoothing the twelve one-dollar notes. The crowd surged around Billy McMahan again. Someone was telling how Brannigan fixed 'em over in the Eleventh. Ikey leaned against the bar a while and then went out.

He went down Hester Street and up Chrystie, and down Delancey to where he lived. And there his womenfolk, a bibulous mother and three dingy sisters, pounced upon him for his wages. And at his confession they shrieked and objurgated him in the pithy rhetoric of the locality.

But even as they plucked at him and struck him, Ikey remained in his ecstatic trance of joy. His head was in the clouds; the star was drawing his wagon. Compared with what he had achieved the loss of wages and the bray of women's tongues were slight affairs.

He had shaken the hand of Billy McMahan.

*   *   *

Billy McMahan had a wife, and upon her visiting cards was engraved the name 'Mrs William Darragh McMahan.' And there was a certain vexation attendant upon these cards; for, small as they were, there were houses in which they could not be inserted. Billy McMahan was a dictator in politics, a four-walled tower in business, a mogul: dreaded, loved and obeyed among his own people. He was growing rich; the daily papers had a dozen men on his trail to chronicle his every word of wisdom; he had been honoured in caricature holding the Tiger cringing in leash.

But the heart of Billy was sometimes sore within him. There was a race of men from which he stood apart but that he viewed with the eye of Moses looking over into the Promised Land. He, too, had ideals, even as had Ikey Snigglefritz; and sometimes, hopeless of attaining them, his own solid success was as dust and ashes in his mouth. And Mrs William Darragh McMahan wore a look of discontent upon her plump but pretty face, and the very rustle of her silks seemed a sigh.

There was a brave and conspicuous assemblage in the dining-saloon of a noted hostelry where Fashion loves to display her charms. At one table sat Billy McMahan and his wife. Mostly silent they were, but the accessories they enjoyed little needed the endorsement of speech. Mrs McMahan's diamonds were outshone by few in the room. The waiter bore the costliest brands of wine to their table. In evening dress, with an expression of gloom upon his smooth and massive countenance, you would look in vain for a more striking figure than Billy's.

Four tables away sat alone a tall, slender man, about thirty, with thoughtful, melancholy eyes, a Van Dyke beard and peculiarly white, thin hands. He was dining on filet mignon, dry toast and apollinaris. That man was Cortlandt Van Duyckink, a man worth eighty millions, who inherited and held a sacred seat in the exclusive inner circle of society.

Billy McMahan spoke to no one around him, because he knew no one. Van Duyckink kept his eyes on his plate because he knew that every eye present was hungry to catch his. He could bestow knighthood and prestige by a nod, and he was chary of creating a too-extensive nobility.

And then Billy McMahan conceived and accomplished the most startling and audacious act of his life. He rose deliberately and walked over to Cortlandt Van Duyckink's table and held out his hand.

'Say, Mr Van Duyckink,' he said. 'I've heard you was talking about starting some reforms among the poor people down in my district. I'm McMahan, you know. Say, now, if that's straight I'll do all I can to help you. And what I says goes in that neck of the woods, don't it? Oh, say, I rather guess it does.'

Van Duyckink's rather sombre eyes lighted up. He rose to his lank height and grasped Billy McMahan's hand.

'Thank you, Mr McMahan,' he said in his deep, serious tones. 'I have been thinking of doing some work of that sort. I shall be glad of your assistance. It pleases me to have become acquainted with you.'

Billy walked back to his seat. His shoulder was tingling from the accolade bestowed by royalty. A hundred eyes were now turned upon him in envy and new admiration. Mrs William Darragh McMahan trembled with ecstasy, so that her diamonds smote the eye almost with pain. And now it was apparent that at many tables there were those who suddenly remembered that they enjoyed Mr McMahan's acquaintance. He saw smiles and bows about him. He became enveloped in the aura of dizzy greatness. His campaign coolness deserted him.

'Wine for that gang!' he commanded the waiter, pointing with his finger. 'Wine over there. Wine to those three gents by that green bush. Tell 'em it's on me. D—n it! Wine for everybody!'

The waiter ventured to whisper that it was perhaps inexpedient to carry out the order, in consideration of the dignity of the house and its custom.

'All right,' said Billy, 'if it's against the rules. I wonder if 'twould do to send my friend Van Duyckink a bottle. No? Well, it'll flow all right at the caffy tonight, just the same. It'll be rubber boots for anybody who comes in there any time up to 2 a.m.'

Billy McMahan was happy.

He had shaken the hand of Cortlandt Van Duyckink.

*   *   *

The big pale-gray auto with its shining metal work looked out of place moving slowly among the push-carts and trash-heaps on the lower East Side. So did Cortlandt Van Duyc-kink, with his aristocratic face and white, thin hands, as he steered carefully between the groups of ragged, scurrying youngsters in the streets. And so did Miss Constance Schuyler, with her dim, ascetic beauty, seated at his side.

'Oh, Cortlandt,' she breathed, 'isn't it sad that human beings have to live in such wretchedness and poverty? And you – how noble it is of you to think of them, to give your time and money to improve their condition!'

Van Duyckink turned his solemn eyes upon her.

'It is little,' he said sadly, 'that I can do. The question is a large one, and belongs to society. But even individual effort is not thrown away. Look, Constance! On this street I have arranged to build soup kitchens, where no one who is hungry will be turned away. And down this other street are the old buildings that I shall cause to be torn down, and there erect others in place of those deathtraps of fire and disease.'

Down Delancey slowly crept the pale-gray auto. Away from it toddled coveys of wondering, tangle-haired, barefooted, unwashed children. It stopped before a crazy brick structure, foul and awry.

Van Duyckink alighted to examine at a better perspective one of the leaning walls. Down the steps of the building came a young man who seemed to epitomise its degradation, squalor and infelicity – a narrow-chested, pale, unsavoury young man, puffing at a cigarette.

Obeying a sudden impulse, Van Duyckink stepped out and warmly grasped the hand of what seemed to him a living rebuke.

'I want to know you people,' he said sincerely. 'I am going to help you as much as I can. We shall be friends.'

As the auto crept carefully away Cortlandt Van Duyckink felt an unaccustomed glow about his heart. He was near to being a happy man

He had shaken the hand of Ikey Snigglefritz.

A Lickpenny Lover

There were 3,000 girls in the Biggest Store. Masie was one of them. She was eighteen, and a sales lady in the gents' gloves. Here she became versed in two varieties of human beings – the kind of gents who buy their gloves in department stores and the kind of women who buy gloves for unfortunate gents. Besides this wide knowledge of the human species, Masie had acquired other information. She had listened to the promulgated wisdom of the 2,999 other girls, and had stored it in a brain that was as secretive and wary as that of a Maltese cat. Perhaps Nature, foreseeing that she would lack wise counsellors, had mingled the saving ingredient of shrewdness along with her beauty, as she has endowed the silver fox of the priceless fur above the other animals with cunning.

For Masie was beautiful. She was a deep-tinted blonde, with the calm poise of a lady who cooks butter-cakes in a window. She stood behind her counter in the Biggest Store; and as you closed your hand over the tape-line for your glove measure you thought of Hebe; and as you looked again you wondered how she had come by Minerva's eyes.

When the floor-walker was not looking Masie chewed tutti frutti; when he was looking she gazed up as if at the clouds and smiled wistfully.

That is the shop-girl smile, and I enjoin you to shun it unless you are well fortified with callosity of the heart, caramels, and a congeniality for the capers of Cupid. This smile belonged to Masie's recreation hours and not to the store; but the floor-walker must have his own. He is the Shy-lock of the stores. When he comes nosing around, the bridge of his nose is a tollbridge. It is goo-goo eyes or 'git' when he looks toward a pretty girl. Of course, not all floor-walkers are thus. Only a few days ago the papers printed news of one over eighty years of age.

One day, Irving Carter, painter, millionaire, traveller, poet, automobilist, happened to enter the Biggest Store. It is due to him to add that his visit was not voluntary. Filial duty took him by the collar and dragged him inside, while his mother philandered among the bronze and terracotta statuettes.

Carter strolled across to the glove counter in order to shoot a few minutes on the wing. His need for gloves was genuine; he had forgotten to bring a pair with him. But his action hardly calls for apology, because he had never heard of glove-counter flirtations.

As he neared the vicinity of his fate he hesitated, suddenly conscious of this unknown phase of Cupid's less worthy profession.

Three or four cheap fellows, sonorously garbed, were leaning over the counters, wrestling with the mediatorial hand-coverings, while giggling girls played vivacious seconds to their lead upon the strident string of coquetry. Carter would have retreated, but he had gone too far. Masie confronted him behind her counter with a questioning look in eyes as coldly, beautifully, warmly blue as the glint of summer sunshine on an iceberg drifting in southern seas.

And then Irving Carter, painter, millionaire, etc., felt a warm flush rise to this aristocratically pale face. But not from diffidence. The blush was intellectual in origin. He knew in a moment that he stood in the ranks of the ready-made youths who wooed the giggling girls at other counters. Himself leaned against the oaken trysting-place of a cockney Cupid with a desire in his heart for the favour of a glove sales girl. He was no more than Bill and Jack and Mickey. And then he felt a sudden tolerance for them, and an elating, courageous contempt for the conventions upon which he had fed, and an unhesitating determination to have this perfect creature for his own.

When the gloves were paid for and wrapped Carter lingered for a moment. The dimples at the corners of Masie's damask mouth deepened. All gentlemen who bought gloves lingered in just that way. She curved an arm, showing like Psyche's through her shirtwaist sleeve, and rested an elbow upon the showcase edge.

Carter had never before encountered a situation of which he had not been perfect master. But now he stood far more awkward than Bill or Jack or Mickey. He had no chance of meeting this beautiful girl socially. His mind struggled to recall the nature and habits of shop-girls as he had read or heard of them. Somehow he had received the idea that they sometimes did not insist too strictly upon the regular channels of introduction. His heart beat loudly at the thought of proposing an unconventional meeting with this lovely and virginal being. But the tumult in his heart gave him courage.

After a few friendly and well-received remarks on general subjects, he laid his card by her hand on the counter.

'Will you please pardon me,' he said, 'if I seem too bold; but I earnestly hope you will allow me the pleasure of seeing you again. There is my name; I assure you that it is with the greatest respect that I ask the favour of becoming one of your fr— acquaintances. May I not hope for the privilege?'

Masie knew men – especially men who buy gloves. Without hesitation she looked him frankly and smilingly in the eyes, and said: 'Sure. I guess you're all right. I don't usually go out with strange gentlemen, though. It ain't quite ladylike. When should you want to see me again?'

'As soon as I may,' said Carter. 'If you would allow me to call at your home, I—'

Masie laughed musically. 'Oh, gee, no!' she said emphatically. 'If you could see our flat once! There's five of us in three rooms. I'd just like to see ma's face if I was to bring a gentleman friend there!'

'Anywhere, then,' said the enamoured Carter, 'that will be convenient to you.'

'Say,' suggested Masie, with a bright-idea look in her peach-blow face, 'I guess Thursday night will about suit me. Suppose you come to the corner of Eighth Avenue and Forty-Eighth Street at 7.30. I live right near the corner. But I've got to be back home by eleven. Ma never lets me stay out after eleven.'

Carter promised gratefully to keep the tryst and then hastened to his mother, who was looking about for him to ratify her purchase of a bronze Diana.

A sales girl, with small eyes and an obtuse nose, strolled near Masie, with a friendly leer.

'Did you make a hit with his nobs, Masie?' she asked familiarly.

'The gentleman asked permission to call,' answered Masie, with the grand air, as she slipped Carter's card into the bosom of her waist.

'Permission to call!' echoed small eyes, with a snigger. 'Did he say anything about dinner in the Waldorf and a spin in his auto afterward?'

'Oh, cheese it!' said Masie wearily. 'You've been used to swell things, I don't think. You've had a swelled head ever since that hose-cart driver took you out to a chop suey joint. No, he never mentioned the Waldorf; but there's a Fifth

Avenue address on his card, and if he buys the supper you can bet your life there won't be no pigtail on the waiter what takes the order.'

As Carter glided away from the Biggest Store with his mother in his electric runabout, he bit his lip with a dull pain at his heart. He knew that love had come to him for the first time in all the twenty-nine years of his life. And that the object of it should make so readily an appointment with him at a street corner, though it was a step toward his desires, tortured him with misgivings.

Carter did not know the shop-girl. He did not know that her home is often either a scarcely habitable, tiny room or a domicile filled to overflowing with kith and kin. The street corner is her parlour, the park is her drawing-room, the avenue is her garden walk; yet for the most part she is as inviolate mistress of herself in them as is my lady inside her tapestried chamber.

One evening at dusk, two weeks after their first meeting, Carter and Masie strolled arm-in-arm into a little, dimly lit park. They found a bench, tree-shadowed and secluded, and sat there.

For the first time his arm stole gently around her. Her golden-bronze head slid restfully against his shoulder.

'Gee!' sighed Masie thankfully. 'Why didn't you ever think of that before?'

'Masie,' said Carter earnestly, 'you surely know that I love you. I ask you sincerely to marry me. You know me well enough by this time to have no doubts of me. I want you, and I must have you. I care nothing for the difference in our stations.'

'What is the difference?' asked Masie curiously.

'Well, there isn't any,' said Carter, quickly, 'except in the minds of foolish people. It is in my power to give you a life of luxury. My social position is beyond dispute, and my means are ample.'

'They all say that,' remarked Masie. 'It's the kid they all give you. I suppose you really work in a delicatessen or follow the races. I ain't as green as I look.'

'I can furnish you all the proofs you want,' said Carter gently. 'And I want you, Masie. I loved you the first day I saw you.'

'They all do,' said Masie, with an amused laugh, 'to hear 'em talk. If I could meet a man that got stuck on me the third time he'd seen me I think I'd get mashed on him.'

'Please don't say such things,' pleaded Carter. 'Listen to me, dear. Ever since I first looked into your eyes you have been the only woman in the world for me.'

'Oh, ain't you the kidder!' smiled Masie. 'How many other girls did you ever tell that?'

But Carter persisted. And at length he reached the flimsy, fluttering little soul of the shop-girl that existed somewhere deep down in her lovely bosom. His words penetrated the heart whose very lightness was its safest armour. She looked up at him with eyes that saw. And a warm glow visited her cool cheeks. Tremblingly, awfully, her moth wings closed, and she seemed about to settle upon the flower of love. Some faint glimmer of life and its possibilities on the other side of her glove counter dawned upon her. Carter felt the change and crowded the opportunity.

'Marry me, Masie,' he whispered softly, 'and we will go away from this ugly city to beautiful ones. We will forget work and business, and life will be one long holiday. I know where I should take you – I have been there often. Just think of a shore where summer is eternal, where the waves are always rippling on the lovely beach and the people are happy and free as children. We will sail to those shores and remain there as long as you please. In one of those faraway cities there are grand and lovely palaces and towers full of beautiful pictures and statues. The streets of the city are water, and one travels about in—'

'I know,' said Masie, sitting up suddenly. 'Gondolas.'

'Yes,' smiled Carter.

'I thought so,' said Masie

'And then,' continued Carter, 'we will travel on and see whatever we wish in the world. After the European cities we will visit India and the ancient cities there, and ride on elephants and see the wonderful temples of the Hindus and Brahmins, and the Japanese gardens, and the camel trains and chariot races in Persia, and all the queer sights of foreign countries. Don't you think you would like it, Masie?'

Masie rose to her feet.

'I think we had better be going home,' she said coolly. 'It's getting late.'

Carter humoured her. He had come to know her varying, thistledown moods, and that it was useless to combat them. But he felt a certain happy triumph. He had held for a moment, though but by a silken thread, the soul of his wild Psyche, and hope was stronger within him. Once she had folded her wings and her cool hand had closed about his own.

At the Biggest Store the next day Masie's chum, Lulu, waylaid her in an angle of the counter.

'How are you and your swell friend making it?' she asked.

'Oh, him?' said Masie, patting her side-curls.' He ain't in it any more. Say, Lu, what do you think that fellow wanted me to do?'

'Go on the stage?' guessed Lulu breathlessly.

'Nit; he's too cheap a guy for that. He wanted me to marry him and go down to Coney Island for a wedding tour!'

The Making of a New Yorker

Besides many other things, Raggles was a poet. He was called a tramp; but that was only an elliptical way of saying that he was a philosopher, an artist, a traveller, a naturalist and a discoverer. But most of all he was a poet. In all his life he never wrote a line of verse; he lived his poetry. His Odyssey would have been a limerick, had it been written. But, to linger with the primary proposition, Raggles was a poet.

Raggles's speciality, had he been driven to ink and paper, would have been sonnets to the cities. He studied cities as women study their reflections in mirrors; as children study the glue and sawdust of a dislocated doll; as the men who write about wild animals study the cages in the zoo. A city to Raggles was not merely a pile of bricks and mortar, peopled by a certain number of inhabitants; it was a thing with a soul characteristic and distinct; an individual conglomeration of life, with its own peculiar essence, flavour and feeling. Two thousand miles to the north and south, east and west, Raggles wandered in poetic fervour, taking the cities to his breast. He footed it on dusty roads, or sped magnificently in freight cars, counting time as of no account. And when he had found the heart of a city and listened to its secret confession, he strayed on, restless, to another. Fickle Raggles! – but perhaps he had not met the civic corporation that could engage and hold his critical fancy.

Through the ancient poets we have learned that the cities are feminine. So they were to poet Raggles; and his mind carried a concrete and clear conception of the figure that symbolised and typified each one that he had wooed.

Chicago seemed to swoop down upon him with a breezy suggestion of Mrs Partington, plumes and patchouli, and to disturb his rest with a soaring and beautiful song of future promise. But Raggles would awake to a sense of shivering cold and a haunting impression of ideals lost in a depressing aura of potato salad and fish.

Thus Chicago affected him. Perhaps there is a vagueness and inaccuracy in the description; but that is Raggles's fault. He should have recorded his sensations in magazine poems.

Pittsburg impressed him as the play of *Othello* performed in the Russian language in a railroad station by Dockstader's minstrels. A royal and generous lady this Pittsburg, though – homely, hearty, with flushed face, washing the dishes in a silk dress and white kid slippers, and bidding Raggles sit before the roaring fireplace and drink champagne with his pigs' feet and fried potatoes.

New Orleans had simply gazed down upon him from a balcony. He could see her pensive, starry eyes and catch the flutter of her fan, and that was all. Only once he came face to face with her. It was at dawn, when she was flushing the red bricks of the banquette with a pail of water. She laughed and hummed a chansonette and filled Raggles's shoes with ice-cold water. *Allons!*

Boston construed herself to the poetic Raggles in an erratic and singular way. It seemed to him that he had drunk cold tea and that the city was a white, cold cloth that had been bound tightly around his brow to spur him to some unknown but tremendous mental effort. And, after all, he came to shovel snow for a livelihood; and the cloth, becoming wet, tightened its knots and could not be removed.

Indefinite and unintelligible ideas, you will say; but your disapprobation should be tempered with gratitude, for these are poets' fancies – and suppose you had come upon them in verse!

One day Raggles came and laid siege to the heart of the great city of Manhattan. She was the greatest of all; and he wanted to learn her note in the scale; to taste and appraise and classify and solve and label her and arrange her with the other cities that had given him up the secret of their individuality. And here we cease to be Raggles's translator and become his chronicler.

Raggles landed from a ferry-boat one morning and walked into the core of the town with the blasé air of a cosmopolite. He was dressed with care to play the role of an 'unidentified man.' No country, race, class, clique, union, party, clan or bowling association could have claimed him. His clothing, which had been donated to him piecemeal by citizens of different height, but same number of inches around the heart, was not yet as uncomfortable to his figure as those specimens of raiment, self-measured, that are railroaded to you by trans-continental tailors with a suitcase, suspenders, silk handkerchief and pearl studs as a bonus. Without money – as a poet should be – but with the ardour of an astronomer discovering a new star in the chorus of the Milky Way, or a man who has seen ink suddenly flow from his fountain pen, Raggles wandered into the great city.

Late in the afternoon he drew out of the roar and commotion with a look of dumb terror on his countenance. He was defeated, puzzled, discomfited, frightened. Other cities had been to him as long primer to read; as country maidens quickly to fathom; as send-price-of-subscription-with-answer rebuses to solve; as oyster cocktails to swallow; but here was one as cold, glittering, serene, impossible as a four-carat diamond in a window to a lover outside fingering damply in his pocket his ribbon-counter salary.

The greetings of the other cities he had known – their home-spun kindliness, their human gamut of rough charity, friendly curses, garrulous curiosity and easily estimated credulity or indifference. This city of Manhattan gave him no clue; it was walled against him. Like a river of adamant it flowed past him in the streets. Never an eye was turned upon him; no voice spoke to him. His heart yearned for the clap of Pittsburg's sooty hand on his shoulder; for Chicago's menacing but social yawp in his ear; for the pale and eleemosynary stare through the Bostonian eyeglass – even for the precipitate but unmalicious boot-toe of Louisville or St Louis.

On Broadway, Raggles, successful suitor of many cities, stood, bashful, like any country swain. For the first time he experienced the poignant humiliation of being ignored. And when he tried to reduce this brilliant, swiftly changing, ice-cold city to a formula he failed utterly. Poet though he was, it offered him no colour, no similes, no points of comparison, no flaw in its polished facets, no handle by which he could hold it up and view its shape and structure, as he familiarly and often contemptuously had done with other towns. The houses were interminable ramparts loopholed for defence; the people were bright but bloodless spectres passing in sinister and selfish array.

The thing that weighed heaviest on Raggles's soul and clogged his poet's fancy was the spirit of absolute egotism that seemed to saturate the people as toys are saturated with paint. Each one that he considered appeared a monster of abominable and insolent conceit. Humanity was gone from them; they were toddling idols of stone and varnish, worshipping themselves and greedy for, though oblivious of, worship from their fellow graven images. Frozen, cruel, implacable, impervious, cut to an identical pattern, they hurried on their ways like statues brought by some miracles to motion, while soul and feeling lay unaroused in the reluctant marble.

Gradually Raggles became conscious of certain types. One was an elderly gentleman with a snow-white short beard, pink unwrinkled face and stony sharp blue eyes, attired in the fashion of a gilded youth, who seemed to personify the city's wealth, ripeness and frigid unconcern. Another type was a woman, tall, beautiful, clear as a steel engraving, goddess-like, calm, clothed like the princesses of old, with eyes as coldly blue as the reflection of sunlight on a glacier. And another was a by-product of this town of marionettes – a broad, swaggering, grim, threateningly sedate fellow, with a jowl as large as a harvested wheatfield, the complexion of a baptised infant and the knuckles of a prizefighter. This type leaned against cigar signs and viewed the world with frapped contumely.

A poet is a sensitive creature, and Raggles soon shrivelled in the bleak embrace of the undecipherable. The chill, sphinx-like, ironical, illegible, unnatural, ruthless expression of the city left him downcast and bewildered. Had it no heart? Better the woodpile, the scolding of vinegar-faced housewives at back doors, the kindly spleen of bartenders behind provincial free-lunch counters, the amiable truculence of rural constables, the kicks, arrests and happy-go-lucky chances of the other vulgar, loud, crude cities than this freezing heartlessness.

Raggles summoned his courage and sought alms from the populace. Unheeding, regardless, they passed on without the wink of an eyelash to testify that they were conscious of his existence. And then he said to himself that this fair but pitiless city of Manhattan was without a soul; that its inhabitants were manikins moved by wires and springs, and that he was alone in a great wilderness.

Raggles started to cross the street. There was a blast, a roar, a hissing and a crash as something struck him and hurled him over and over six yards from where he had been. As he was coming down like the stick of a rocket the earth and all the cities thereof turned to a fractured dream.

Raggles opened his eyes. First an odour made itself known to him – an odour of the earliest spring flowers of Paradise. And then a hand soft as a falling petal touched his brow. Bending over him was the woman clothed like the princess of old, with blue eyes, now soft and humid with human sympathy. Under his head on the pavement were silks and furs. With Raggles's hat in his hand and with his face pinker than ever from a vehement burst of oratory against reckless driving, stood the elderly gentleman who personified the city's wealth and ripeness. From a nearby café hurried the by-product with the vast jowl and baby complexion, bearing a glass full of a crimson fluid that suggested delightful possibilities.

'Drink dis, sport,' said the by-product, holding the glass to Raggles's lips.

Hundreds of people huddled around in a moment, their faces wearing the deepest concern. Two flattering and gorgeous policemen got into the circle and pressed back the overplus of Samaritans. An old lady in a black shawl spoke loudly of camphor; a newsboy slipped one of his papers beneath Raggles's elbow, where it lay on the muddy pavement. A brisk young man with a notebook was asking for names.

A bell clanged importantly, and the ambulance cleared a lane through the crowd. A cool surgeon slipped into the midst of affairs.

'How do you feel, old man?' asked the surgeon, stooping easily to his task. The princess of silks and satins wiped a red drop or two from Raggles's brow with a fragrant cobweb.

'Me?' said Raggles, with a seraphic smile. 'I feel fine.'

He had found the heart of his new city.

In three days they let him leave his cot for the convalescent ward in the hospital. He had been in there an hour when the attendants heard sounds of conflict. Upon investigation they found that Raggles had assaulted and damaged a brother convalescent – a glowering transient whom a freight train collision had sent in to be patched up.

'What's all this about?' enquired the head nurse.

'He was runnin' down me town,' said Raggles

'What town?' asked the nurse.

'Noo York,' said Raggles.

The Buyer from Cactus City

It is well that hay fever and colds do not obtain in the healthful vicinity of Cactus City, Texas, for the dry goods emporium of Navarro & Platt, situated there, is not to be sneezed at.

Twenty thousand people in Cactus City scatter their silver coin with liberal hands for the things that their hearts desire. The bulk of this semi-precious metal goes to Navarro & Platt. Their huge brick building covers enough ground to graze a dozen head of sheep. You can buy of them a rattlesnake-skin necktie, an automobile, or an eighty-five-dollar, latest style, ladies' tan coat in twenty different shades. Navarro & Platt first introduced pennies west of the Colorado River. They had been ranchmen with business heads, who saw that the world did not necessarily have to cease its revolutions after free grass went out.

Every spring, Navarro, senior partner, fifty-five, half Spanish, cosmopolitan, able, polished, had 'gone on' to New York to buy goods. This year he shied at taking up the long trail. He was undoubtedly growing older; and he looked at his watch several times a day before the hour came for his siesta.

'John,' he said, to his junior partner, 'you shall go on this year to buy the goods.'

Platt looked tired.

'I'm told,' said he, 'that New York is a plumb dead town; but I'll go. I can take a whirl in San Antone for a few days on my way and have some fun.'

Two weeks later a man in a Texas full dress suit – black

49

frock-coat, broad-brimmed, soft, white hat, and lay-down collar 3–4 inch high, with black, wrought-iron necktie – entered the wholesale cloak and suit establishment of Zizzbaum & Son, on Lower Broadway.

Old Zizzbaum had the eye of an osprey, the memory of an elephant and a mind that unfolded from him in three movements like the puzzle of the carpenter's rule. He rolled to the front like a brunette polar bear, and shook Platt's hand.

'And how is the good Mr Navarro in Texas?' he said. 'The trip was too long for him this year, so? We welcome Mr Platt instead.'

'A bull's-eye,' said Platt, 'and I'd give forty acres of unirrigated Pecos County land to know how you did it.'

'I knew,' grinned Zizzbaum, 'just as I know that the rainfall in El Paso for the year was 28.5 inches, or an increase of 15 inches, and that therefore Navarro & Platt will buy a $15,000 stock of suits this spring instead of $10,000, as in a dry year. But that will be tomorrow. There is first a cigar in my private office that will remove from your mouth the taste of the ones you smuggle across the Rio Grande and like – because they are smuggled.'

It was late in the afternoon and business for the day had ended, Zizzbaum left Platt with a half-smoked cigar and came out of the private office to Son, who was arranging his diamond scarf pin before a mirror, ready to leave.

'Abey,' he said, 'you will have to take Mr Platt around tonight and show him things. They are customers for ten years. Mr Navarro and I we played chess every moment of spare time when he came. That is good, but Mr Platt is a young man and this is his first visit to New York. He should amuse easily.'

'All right,' said Abey, screwing the guard tightly on his pin.

'I'll take him on. After he's seen the Flatiron and the head waiter at the Hotel Astor and heard the phonograph play "Under The Old Apple Tree" it'll be half-past ten, and Mr Texas will be ready to roll up in his blanket. I've got a supper engagement at 11.30, but he'll be all to the Mrs Winslow before then.'

The next morning at ten Platt walked into the store ready to do business. He had a bunch of hyacinths pinned on his lapel. Zizzbaum himself waited on him. Navarro & Platt were good customers, and never failed to take their discount for cash.

'And what did you think of our little town?' asked Zizzbaum, with the fatuous smile of the Manhattanite.

'I shouldn't care to live in it,' said the Texan. 'Your son and I knocked around quite a little last night. You've got good water, but Cactus City is better lit up.'

'We've got a few lights on Broadway, don't you think, Mr Platt?'

'And a good many shadows,' said Platt. 'I think I like your horses best. I haven't seen a crowbait since I've been in town.'

Zizzbaum led him upstairs to show the samples of suits.

'Ask Miss Asher to come,' he said to a clerk.

Miss Asher came, and Platt, of Navarro & Platt, felt for the first time the wonderful bright light of romance and glory descend upon him. He stood still as a granite cliff above the canon of the Colorado, with his wide-open eyes fixed upon her. She noticed his look and flushed a little, which was contrary to her custom.

Miss Asher was the crack model of Zizzbaum & Son. She was of the blonde type known as 'medium', and her measurements even went the required 38–25–42 standard a little better. She had been at Zizzbaum's two years, and knew her business. Her eye was bright, but cool; and had she chosen to match her gaze against the optic of the famed basilisk, that fabulous monster's gaze would have wavered and softened first. Incidentally, she knew buyers.

'Now, Mr Platt,' said Zizzbaum, 'I want you to see these princesse gowns in the light shades. They will be the thing in your climate. This first, if you please, Miss Asher.'

Swiftly in and out of the dressing-room the prize model flew, each time wearing a new costume and looking more stunning with every change. She posed with absolute self-possession before the stricken buyer, who stood, tongue-tied and motionless, while Zizzbaum orated oilily of the styles. On the model's face was her faint, impersonal professional smile that seemed to cover something like weariness or contempt.

When the display was over Platt seemed to hesitate. Zizzbaum was a little anxious, thinking that his customer might be inclined to try elsewhere. But Platt was only looking over in his mind the best building sites in Cactus City, trying to select one on which to build a house for his wife-to-be – who was just then in the dressing-room taking off an evening gown of lavender and tulle.

'Take your time, Mr Platt,' said Zizzbaum. 'Think it over tonight. You won't find anybody else meet our prices on goods like these. I'm afraid you're having a dull time in New York, Mr Platt. A young man like you – of course, you miss the society of the ladies. Wouldn't you like a nice young lady to take out to dinner this evening? Miss Asher, now, is a very nice young lady; she will make it agreeable for you.'

'Why, she doesn't know me,' said Platt wonderingly. 'She doesn't know anything about me. Would she go? I'm not acquainted with her.'

'Would she go?' repeated Zizzbaum, with uplifted eyebrows.

'Sure, she would go. I will introduce you. Sure, she would go.'

He called Miss Asher loudly.

She came, calm and slightly contemptuous, in her white shirtwaist and plain black shirt.

'Mr Platt would like the pleasure of your company to dinner this evening,' said Zizzbaum, walking away.

'Sure,' said Miss Asher, looking at the ceiling. 'I'd be much pleased. Nine-eleven West Twentieth Street. What time?'

'Say seven o'clock.'

'All right, but please don't come ahead of time. I room with a schoolteacher, and she doesn't allow any gentlemen to call in the room. There isn't any parlour, so you'll have to wait in the hall. I'll be ready.'

At half-past seven Platt and Miss Asher sat at a table in a Broadway restaurant. She was dressed in a plain filmy black. Platt didn't know that it was all a part of her day's work.

With the unobtrusive aid of a good waiter he managed to order a respectable dinner, minus the usual Broadway preliminaries.

Miss Asher flashed upon him a dazzling smile.

'Mayn't I have something to drink?' she asked.

'Why, certainly,' said Platt. 'Anything you want.'

'A dry Martini,' she said to the waiter.

When it was brought and set before her Platt reached over and took it away. 'What is this?' he asked.

'A cocktail, of course.'

'I thought it was some kind of tea you ordered. This is liquor. You can't drink this. What is your first name?'

'To my intimate friends,' said Miss Asher freezingly, 'it is "Helen".'

'Listen, Helen,' said Platt, leaning over the table. 'For many years every time the spring flowers blossomed out on the prairies I got to thinking of somebody that I'd never seen or heard of. I knew it was you the minute I saw you yesterday. I'm going back home tomorrow and you're going with me. I know it, for I saw it in your eyes when you first looked at me. You needn't kick, for you've got to fall into line. Here's a little trick I picked out for you on my way over.'

He flicked a two-carat diamond solitaire ring across the table. Miss Asher flipped it back to him with her fork.

'Don't get fresh,' she said severely.

'I'm worth a hundred thousand dollars,' said Platt. 'I'll build you the finest house in West Texas.'

'You can't buy me, Mr Buyer,' said Miss Asher, 'if you had a hundred million. I didn't think I'd have to call you down. You didn't look like the others to me at first, but I see you're all alike.'

'All who?' asked Platt.

'All you buyers. You think because we girls have to go out to dinner with you or lose our jobs that you're privileged to say what you please. Well, forget it. I thought you were different from the others, but I see I was mistaken.'

Platt struck his fingers on the table with a gesture of sudden, illuminating satisfaction.

'I've got it!' he exclaimed, almost hilariously – 'the Nicholson place, over on the north side. There's a big grove of live oaks and a natural lake. The old house can be pulled down and the new one set farther back.'

'Put out your pipe,' said Miss Asher. 'I'm sorry to wake you up, but you fellows might as well get wise, once for all, to where you stand. I'm supposed to go to dinner with you and help jolly you along so you'll trade with old Zizzy, but don't expect to find me in any of the suits you buy.'

'Do you mean to tell me,' said Platt, 'that you go out this

way with customers, and they all – they all talk to you like I have?'

'They all make plays,' said Miss Asher. 'But I must say that you've got 'em beat in one respect. They generally talk diamonds while you've actually dug one up.'

'How long have you been working, Helen?'

'Got my name pat, haven't you? I've been supporting myself for eight years. I was a cash girl, and a wrapper, and then a shop-girl until I was grown, and then I got to be a suit model. Mr Texas Man, don't you think a little wine would make this dinner a little less dry?'

'You're not going to drink wine any more, dear. It's awful to think how – I'll come to the store tomorrow and get you. I want you to pick out an automobile before we leave. That's all we need to buy here.'

'Oh, cut that out. If you knew how sick I am of hearing such talk.'

After the dinner they walked down Broadway and came upon Diana's little wooded park. The trees caught Platt's eye at once, and he must turn along under the winding walk beneath them. The lights shone upon two bright tears in the model's eyes.

'I don't like that,' said Platt. 'What's the matter?'

'Don't you mind,' said Miss Asher. 'Well, it's because – well, I didn't think you were that kind when I first saw you. But you are all alike. And now will you take me home, or will I have to call a cop?'

Platt took her to the door of her boarding-house. They stood for a minute in the vestibule. She looked at him with such scorn in her eyes that even his heart of oak began to waver. His arm was halfway around her waist, when she struck him a stinging blow on the face with her open hand.

As he stepped back a ring fell from somewhere and bounded

on the tiled floor. Platt groped for it and found it.

'Now, take your useless diamond and go, Mr Buyer,' she said.

'This was the other one – the wedding ring,' said the Texan, holding the smooth, gold band on the palm of his hand.

Miss Asher's eyes blazed upon him in the half darkness.

'Was that what you meant? – did you—'

Somebody opened the door from inside the house.

'Good night,' said Platt. 'I'll see you at the store tomorrow.'

Miss Asher ran up to her room and shook the schoolteacher until she sat up in bed ready to scream 'Fire!'

'Where is it?' she cried.

'That's what I want to know,' said the model. 'You've studied geography, Emma, and you ought to know. Where is a town called Cac – Cac – Carac – Caracas City, I think they called it?'

'How dare you wake me up for that?' said the schoolteacher. 'Caracas is in Venezuela, of course.'

'What's it like?'

'Why, it's principally earthquakes and negroes and monkeys and malarial fever and volcanoes.'

'I don't care,' said Miss Asher blithely; 'I'm going there tomorrow.'

Springtime à la Carte

It was a day in March.

Never, never begin a story this way when you write one. No opening could possibly be worse. It is unimaginative, flat, dry and likely to consist of mere wind. But in this instance it is allowable. For the following paragraph, which should have inaugurated the narrative, is too wildly extravagant and preposterous to be flaunted in the face of the reader without preparation.

Sarah was crying over her bill of fare.

Think of a New York girl shedding tears on the menu card!

To account for this you will be allowed to guess that the lobsters were all out, or that she had sworn ice cream off during Lent, or that she had ordered onions, or that she had just come from a Hackett matinée. And then, all these theories being wrong, you will please let the story proceed.

The gentleman who announced that the world was an oyster which he with his sword would open made a larger hit than he deserved. It is not difficult to open an oyster with a sword. But did you ever notice anyone try to open the terrestrial bivalve with a typewriter? Like to wait for a dozen raw opened that way?

Sarah had managed to pry apart the shells with her unhandy weapon far enough to nibble a wee bit at the cold and clammy world within. She knew no more shorthand than if she had been a graduate in stenography just let slip upon the world by a business college. So, not being able to stenog, she could not enter that bright galaxy of office talent. She was a freelance typewriter and canvassed for odd jobs of copying.

The most brilliant and crowning feat of Sarah's battle with the world was the deal she made with Schulenberg's Home Restaurant. The restaurant was next door to the old red brick in which she hall-roomed. One evening after dining at Schulenberg's forty-cent five-course *table d'hôte* (served as fast as you throw the five baseballs at the coloured gentleman's head) Sarah took away with her the bill of fare. It was written in an almost unreadable script neither English nor German, and so arranged that if you were not careful you began with a toothpick and rice pudding and ended with soup and the day of the week.

The next day Sarah showed Schulenberg a neat card on which the menu was beautifully typewritten with the viands temptingly marshalled under their right and proper heads from 'hors d'oeuvre' to 'not responsible for overcoats and umbrellas.'

Schulenberg became a naturalised citizen on the spot. Before Sarah left him she had him willingly committed to an agreement. She was to furnish typewritten bills of fare for the twenty-one tables in the restaurant – a new bill for each day's dinner, and new ones for breakfast and lunch as often as changes occurred in the food or as neatness required.

In return for this Schulenberg was to send three meals *per diem* to Sarah's hall-room by a waiter – an obsequious one if possible – and furnish her each afternoon with a pencil draft of what Fate had in store for Schulenberg's customers on the morrow.

Mutual satisfaction resulted from the agreement. Schulenberg's patrons now knew what the food they ate was called even if its nature sometimes puzzled them. And Sarah had food during a cold, dull winter, which was the main thing with her.

And then the almanac lied, and said that spring had come.

Spring comes when it comes. The frozen snows of January still lay like adamant in the cross-town streets. The hand-organs still played 'In The Good Old Summertime', with their December vivacity and expression. Men began to make thirty-day notes to buy Easter dresses. Janitors shut off steam. And when these things happen one may know that the city is still in the clutches of winter.

One afternoon Sarah shivered in her elegant hall-bedroom; 'house heated; scrupulously clean; conveniences; seen to be appreciated.' She had no work to do except Schulenberg's menu cards. Sarah sat in her squeaky willow rocker, and looked out the window. The calendar on the wall kept crying to her: 'Springtime is here, Sarah – springtime is here, I tell you. Look at me, Sarah, my figures show it. You've got a neat figure yourself, Sarah – a nice, springtime figure – why do you look out the window so sadly?'

Sarah's room was at the back of the house. Looking out the window she could see the windowless rear brick wall of the box factory on the next street. But the wall was clearest crystal; and Sarah was looking down a grassy lane shaded with cherry trees and elms and bordered with raspberry bushes and Cherokee roses.

Spring's real harbingers are too subtle for the eye and ear. Some must have the flowering crocus, the wood-starring dogwood, the voice of bluebird – even so gross a reminder as the farewell handshake of the retiring buckwheat and oyster before they can welcome the Lady in Green to their dull bosoms. But to old earth's choicest kin there come straight, sweet messages from his newest bride, telling them they shall be no stepchildren unless they choose to be.

On the previous summer Sarah had gone into the country and loved a farmer.

(In writing your story never hark back thus. It is bad art, and cripples interest. Let it march, march.)

Sarah stayed two weeks at Sunnybrook Farm. There she learned to love old Farmer Franklin's son, Walter. Farmers have been loved and wedded and turned out to grass in less time. But young Walter Franklin was a modern agriculturist. He had a telephone in his cowhouse, and he could figure up exactly what effect next year's Canada wheat crop would have on potatoes planted in the dark of the moon.

It was in this shaded and raspberried lane that Walter had wooed and won her. And together they had sat and woven a crown of dandelions for her hair. He had immoderately praised the effect of the yellow blossoms against her brown tresses; and she had left the chaplet there, and walked back to the house swinging her straw sailor in her hands.

They were to marry in the spring – at the very first signs of spring, Walter said. And Sarah came back to the city to pound her typewriter.

A knock at the door dispelled Sarah's visions of that happy day. A waiter had brought the rough pencil draft of the Home Restaurant's next day fare in old Schulenberg's angular hand.

Sarah sat down at her typewriter and slipped a card between the rollers. She was a nimble worker. Generally in an hour and a half the twenty-one menu cards were written and ready.

Today there were more changes on the bill of fare than usual. The soups were lighter; pork was eliminated from the entrees, figuring only with Russian turnips among the roasts. The gracious spirit of spring pervaded the entire menu. Lamb, that lately capered on the greening hillsides, was becoming exploited with the sauce that commemorated its gambols. The song of the oyster, though not silenced, was *diminuendo con amore*. The frying-pan seemed to be held, inactive, behind the beneficent bars of the broiler. The pie list swelled; the richer puddings had vanished; the sausage, with his drapery wrapped about him, barely lingered in a pleasant thanatopsis with the buckwheats and the sweet but doomed maple.

Sarah's fingers danced like midgets above a summer stream. Down through the courses she worked, giving each item its position according to its length with an accurate eye.

Just above the desserts came the list of vegetables. Carrots and peas, asparagus on toast, the perennial tomatoes and corn and succotash, lima beans, cabbage – and then –

Sarah was crying over her bill of fare. Tears from the depths of some divine despair rose in her heart and gathered to her eyes. Down went her head on the little typewriter stand; and the keyboard rattled a dry accompaniment to her moist sobs.

For she had received no letter from Walter in two weeks, and the next item on the bill of fare was dandelions – dandelions with some kind of egg – but bother the egg! – dandelions, with whose golden blooms Walter had crowned her his queen of love and future bride – dandelions, the harbingers of spring, her sorrow's crown of sorrow – reminder of her happiest days.

Madam, I dare you to smile until you suffer this test: let the Marèchal Niel roses that Percy brought you on the night you gave him your heart be served as a salad with French dressing before your eyes at a Schulenberg *table d'hôte*. Had Juliet so seen her love tokens dishonoured the sooner would she have sought the lethean herbs of the good apothecary.

But what a witch is Spring! Into the great cold city of stone and iron a message had to be sent. There was none to convey it but the little hardy courier of the fields with his rough, green coat and modest air. He is a true soldier of fortune, this *dent-de-lion* – this lion's tooth, as the French chefs call him. Flowered, he will assist at love-making, wreathed in my lady's nut-brown hair; young and callow and unblossomed, he goes into the boiling pot and delivers the word of his sovereign mistress.

By and by Sarah forced back her tears. The cards must be written. But, still in a faint, golden glow from her dandeleonine dream, she fingered the typewriter keys absently for a little while, with her mind and heart in the meadow lane with her young farmer. But soon she came swiftly back to the rockbound lanes of Manhattan, and the typewriter began to rattle and jump like a strike-breaker's motor car.

At six o'clock the waiter brought her dinner and carried away the typewritten bill of fare. When Sarah ate she set aside, with a sigh, the dish of dandelions with its crowning ovarious accompaniment. As this dark mass had been transformed from a bright and love-endorsed flower to be an ignominious vegetable, so had her summer hopes wilted and perished. Love may, as Shakespeare said, feed on itself: but Sarah could not bring herself to eat the dandelions that had graced, as ornaments, the first spiritual banquet of her heart's true affection.

At 7.30 the couple in the next room began to quarrel; the man in the room above sought for A on his flute; the gas went a little lower; three coal wagons started to unload – the only sound of which the phonograph is jealous; cats on the back fences slowly retreated toward Mukden. By these signs Sarah knew that it was time for her to read. She got out *The Cloister and the Hearth,* the best non-selling book of the month, settled her feet on her trunk, and began to wander with Gerard.

The front-doorbell rang. The landlady answered it. Sarah left Gerard and Denys treed by a bear and listened. Oh, yes; you would, just as she did!

And then a strong voice was heard in the hall below, and Sarah jumped for her door, leaving the book on the floor and the first round easily the bear's.

You have guessed it. She reached the top of the stairs just as her farmer came up, three at a jump, and reaped and garnered her, with nothing left for the gleaners.

'Why haven't you written – oh, why?' cried Sarah.

'New York is a pretty large town,' said Walter Fanklin. I came in a week ago to your old address. I found that you went away on a Thursday. That consoled some; it eliminated the possible Friday bad luck. But it didn't prevent my hunting for you with police and otherwise ever since!'

'I wrote!' said Sarah vehemently

'Never got it!'

'Then how did you find me?'

The young farmer smiled a springtime smile.

'I dropped into that Home Restaurant next door this evening,' said he. 'I don't care who knows it; I like a dish of some kind of greens at this time of the year. I ran my eye down that nice, typewritten bill of fare looking for something in that line. When I got below cabbage I turned my chair over and hollered for the proprietor. He told me where you lived.'

'I remember,' sighed Sarah happily. 'That was dandelions below cabbage.'

'I'd know that cranky capital W 'way above the line that your typewriter makes anywhere in the world,' said Franklin.

'Why, there's no W in dandelions,' said Sarah, in surprise.

The young man drew the bill of fare from his pocket, and pointed to a line.

Sarah recognised the first card she had typewritten that afternoon. There was still the rayed splotch in the upper right-hand corner where a tear had fallen. But over the spot where one should have read the name of the meadow plant, the clinging memory of their golden blossoms had allowed her fingers to strike strange keys.

Between the red cabbage and the stuffed green peppers was the item:

'DEAREST WALTER, WITH HARD-BOILED EGG.'

The Third Ingredient

The (so-called) Vallambrosa Apartment House is not an apartment-house. It is composed of two old-fashioned, brownstone-front residences welded into one. The parlour floor of one side is gay with the wraps and headgear of a modiste; the other is lugubrious with the sophistical promises and grisly display of a painless dentist. You may have a room there for two dollars a week or you may have one for twenty dollars. Among the Vallambrosa's roomers are stenographers, musicians, brokers, shop-girls, space-rate writers, art students, wire-tappers, and other people who lean far over the banister-rail when the doorbell rings.

This treatise shall have to do with two of the Vallambrosians – though meaning no disrespect to the others.

At six o'clock one afternoon Hetty Pepper came back to her third-floor-rear three-dollar-fifty-cent room in the Vallambrosa with her nose and chin more sharply pointed than usual. To be discharged from the department store where you have been working four years, and with only fifteen cents in your purse, does have a tendency to make your features appear more finely chiselled.

And now for Hetty's thumbnail biography while she climbs the two flights of stairs.

She walked into the Biggest Store one morning four years before, with seventy-five other girls, applying for a job behind the waist department counter. The phalanx of wage-earners formed a bewildering scene of beauty, carrying a total mass of blonde hair sufficient to have justified the horseback gallops of a hundred Lady Godivas.

The capable, cool-eyed, impersonal, young, bald-headed man, whose task it was to engage six of the contestants, was aware of a feeling of suffocation as if he were drowning in a sea of frangipanni, while white clouds, hand-embroidered, floated about him. And then a sail hove in sight. Hetty Pepper, homely of countenance, with small, contemptuous, green eyes and chocolate-coloured hair, dressed in a suit of plain burlap and a common-sense hat, stood before him with every one of her twenty-nine years of life unmistakably in sight.

'You're on!' shouted the bald-headed young man, and was saved. And that is how Hetty came to be employed in the Biggest Store. The story of her rise to an eight-dollar-a-week salary is the combined stories of Hercules, Joan of Arc, Una, Job, and Little Red Riding Hood. You shall not learn from me the salary that was paid her as a beginner. There is a sentiment growing about such things, and I want no millionaire store-proprietors climbing the fire escape of my tenement-house to throw dynamite bombs into my skylight boudoir.

The story of Hetty's discharge from the Biggest Store is so nearly a repetition of her engagement as to be monotonous.

In each department of the store there is an omniscient, omnipresent and omnivorous person carrying always a mileage book and a red necktie, and referred to as a 'buyer'. The destinies of the girls in his department who live on (see Bureau of Victual Statistics) – so much per week are in his hands.

This particular buyer was a capable, cool-eyed, impersonal, young, bald-headed man. As he walked along the aisles of his department he seemed to be sailing on a sea of frangipanni, while white clouds, machine-embroidered, floated around

66

him. Too many sweets bring surfeit. He looked upon Hetty Pepper's homely countenance, emerald eyes, and chocolate-coloured hair as a welcome oasis of green in a desert of cloying beauty. In a quiet angle of a counter he pinched her arm kindly, three inches above the elbow. She slapped him three feet away with one good blow of her muscular and not especially lily-white right. So, now you know why Hetty Pepper came to leave the Biggest Store at thirty minutes' notice, with one dime and a nickel in her purse.

This morning's quotations list the price of rib beef at six cents per (butcher's) pound. But on the day that Hetty was 'released' by the B.S. the price was seven and one-half cents. That fact is what makes this story possible. Otherwise the extra four cents would have –

But the plot of nearly all the good stories in the world is concerned with shorts who were unable to cover; so you can find no fault with this one.

Hetty mounted with her rib beef to her three-dollar-fifty-cent third-floor-back. One hot, savoury beef-stew for supper, a night's good sleep, and she would be fit in the morning to apply again for the tasks of Hercules, Joan of Arc, Una, Job, and Little Red Riding Hood.

In her room she got the graniteware stew-pan out of the 2 by 4-foot china – er – I mean earthenware closet, and began to dig down in a rat's-nest of paper bags for the potatoes and onions. She came out with her nose and chin just a little sharper pointed.

There was neither a potato nor an onion. Now, what kind of beef-stew can you make out of simply beef? You can make oyster-soup without oysters, turtle-soup without turtles, coffee-cake without coffee, but you can't make beef-stew without potatoes and onions.

But rib beef alone, in an emergency, can make an ordinary pine door look like a wrought-iron gambling-house portal to the wolf. With salt and pepper and a tablespoonful of flour (first well stirred in a little cold water) 'twill serve – 'tis not so deep as a lobster a la Newburgh, nor so wide as a church festival doughnut; but 'twill serve.

Hetty took her stew-pan to the rear of the third-floor hall. According to the advertisements of the Vallambrosa there was running water to be found there. Between you and me and the water-meter, it only ambled or walked through the faucets; but technicalities have no place here. There was also a sink where housekeeping roomers often met to dump their coffee grounds and glare at one another's kimonos.

At this sink Hetty found a girl with heavy, gold-brown artistic hair and plaintive eyes, washing two large 'Irish' potatoes. Hetty knew the Vallambrosa as well as anyone not owning 'double hextra-magnifying eyes' could compass its mysteries. The kimonos were her encyclopaedia, her 'Who's What?' her clearing-house of news, of goers and comers. From a rose-pink kimono edged with Nile green she had learned that the girl with the potatoes was a miniature-painter living in a kind of attic – or 'studio', as they prefer to call it – on the top floor. Hetty was not certain in her mind what a miniature was; but it certainly wasn't a house; because house-painters, although they wear splashy overalls and poke ladders in your face on the street, are known to indulge in a riotous profusion of food at home.

The potato girl was quite slim and small, and handled her potatoes as an old bachelor uncle handles a baby who is cutting teeth. She had a dull shoemaker's knife in her right hand, and she had begun to peel one of the potatoes with it.

Hetty addressed her in the punctiliously formal tone of one

who intends to be cheerfully familiar with you in the second round.

'Beg pardon,' she said, 'for butting into what's not my business, but if you peel them potatoes you lose out. They're new Bermudas. You want to scrape 'em. Lemme show you.'

She took a potato and the knife and began to demonstrate.

'Oh, thank you,' breathed the artist. 'I didn't know. And I *did* hate to see the thick peeling go; it seemed such a waste. But I thought they always had to be peeled. When you've got only potatoes to eat, the peelings count, you know.'

'Say, kid,' said Hetty, staying her knife, 'you ain't up against it, too, are you?'

The miniature artist smiled stonedly.

'I suppose I am. Art – or, at least, the way I interpret it – doesn't seem to be much in demand. I have only these potatoes for my dinner. But they aren't so bad boiled and hot, with a little butter and salt.'

'Child,' said Hetty, letting a brief smile soften her rigid features, 'Fate has sent me and you together. I've had it handed to me in the neck, too; but I've got a chunk of meat in my room as big as a lapdog. And I've done everything to get potatoes except pray for 'em. Let's me and you bunch our commissary departments and make a stew of 'em. We'll cook it in my room. If we only had an onion to go in it! Say, kid, you haven't got a couple of pennies that've slipped down into the lining of your last winter's sealskin, have you? I could step down to the corner and get one at old Giuseppe's stand. A stew without an onion is worse'n a matinee without candy.'

'You may call me Cecilia,' said the artist. 'No; I spent my last penny three days ago.'

'Then we'll have to cut the onion out instead of slicing it in,' said Hetty. 'I'd ask the janitress for one, but I don't want 'em hep just yet to the fact that I'm pounding the asphalt for another job. But I wish we did have an onion.'

In the shop-girl's room the two began to prepare their supper. Cecilia's part was to sit on the couch helplessly and beg to be allowed to do something in the voice of a cooing ringdove. Hetty prepared the rib beef, putting it in cold salted water in the stew-pan and setting it on the one-burner gas-stove.

'I wish we had an onion,' said Hetty, as she scraped the two potatoes.

On the wall opposite the couch was pinned a flaming, gorgeous advertising picture of one of the new ferryboats of the P.U.F.F. Railroad that had been built to cut down the time between Los Angeles and New York City one eighth of a minute.

Hetty turned her head during her continuous monologue, saw tears running from her guest's eyes as she gazed on the idealised presentment of the speeding, foam-girdled transport.

'Why, say, Cecilia, kid,' said Hetty, poising her knife, 'is it as bad art as that? I ain't a critic, but I thought it kind of brightened up the room. Of course, a manicure-painter could tell it was a bum picture in a minute. I'll take it down, if you say so; I wish to the holy St Pot-Luck we had an onion.'

But the miniature miniature-painter had tumbled down, sobbing, with her nose indenting the hard-woven drapery of the couch. Something was here deeper than the artistic temperament offended at crude lithography.

Hetty knew. She had accepted her role long ago. How scant the words with which we try to describe a single quality of a human being! When we reach the abstract we are lost. The nearer to Nature that the babbling of our lips comes, the better do we understand. Figuratively (let us say), some people are Bosoms, some are Hands, some are Heads, some are Muscles, some are Feet, some are Backs for burdens.

Hetty was a Shoulder. Hers was a sharp, sinewy shoulder; but all her life people had laid their heads upon it, metaphorically or actually and had left there all or half their troubles. Looking at Life anatomically, which is as good a way as any, she was pre-ordained to be a Shoulder. There were few truer collarbones anywhere than hers.

Hetty was only thirty-three, and she had not yet outlived the little pang that visited her whenever the head of youth and beauty leaned upon her for consolation. But one glance in her mirror always served as an instantaneous painkiller. So she gave one pale look into the crinkly old looking-glass on the wall above the gas-stove, turned down the flame a little lower from the bubbling beef and potatoes, went over to the couch, and lifted Cecilia's head to its confessional.

'Go on and tell me, honey,' she said. 'I know now that it ain't art that's worrying you. You met him on a ferry-boat, didn't you? Go on, Cecilia, kid, and tell your – your Aunt Hetty about it.'

But youth and melancholy must first spend the surplus of sighs and tears that waft and float the barque of romance to its harbour in the delectable isles. Presently, through the stringy tendons that formed the bars of the confessional, the penitent – or was it the glorified communicant of the sacred flame? – told her story without art or illumination.

'It was only three days ago. I was coming back on the ferry from Jersey City. Old Mr Schrum, an art dealer, told me of a rich man in Newark who wanted a miniature of his daughter painted. I went to see him and showed him some of my work. When I told him the price would be fifty dollars he laughed at me like a hyena. He said an enlarged crayon twenty times the size would cost him only eight dollars.

'I had just enough money to buy my ferry ticket back to New York. I felt as if I didn't want to live another day. I must have looked as I felt, for I saw him on the row of seats opposite me, looking at me as if he understood. He was nice-looking, but, oh, above everything else, he looked kind. When one is tired or unhappy or hopeless, kindness counts more than anything else.

'When I got so miserable that I couldn't fight against it any longer, I got up and walked out of the rear door of the ferry-boat cabin. No one was there, and I slipped quickly over the rail, and dropped into the water. Oh, friend Hetty, it was cold, cold!

'For just one moment I wished I was back in the old Vallambrosa, starving and hoping. And then I got numb, and didn't care. And then I felt that somebody else was in the water close by me, holding me up. *He* had followed me, and jumped in to save me.

'Somebody threw a thing like a big, white doughnut at us, and he made me put my arms through the hole. Then the ferry-boat backed, and they pulled us on board. Oh, Hetty, I was so ashamed of my wickedness in trying to drown myself; and, besides, my hair had all tumbled down and was sopping wet, and I was such a sight.

'And then some men in blue clothes came around; and *he* gave them his card, and I heard him tell them he had seen me drop my purse on the edge of the boat outside the rail, and in leaning over to get it I had fallen overboard. And then I remembered having read in the papers that people who try to kill themselves are locked up in cells with people who try to kill other people, and I was afraid.

'But some ladies on the boat took me downstairs to the

furnace-room and got me nearly dry and did up my hair. When the boat landed, *he* came and put me in a cab. He was all dripping himself, but laughed as if he thought it was all a joke. He begged me, but I wouldn't tell him my name nor where I lived, I was so ashamed.'

'You were a fool, child,' said Hetty, kindly. 'Wait till I turn up the light a bit. I wish to Heaven we had an onion.'

'Then he raised his hat,' went on Cecilia, 'and said: "Very well. But I'll find you, anyhow. I'm going to claim my rights of salvage." Then he gave money to the cab-driver and told him to take me where I wanted to go, and walked away. What is "salvage", Hetty?'

'The edge of a piece of goods that ain't hemmed,' said the shop-girl. 'You must have looked pretty well frazzled out to the little hero boy.'

'It's been three days,' moaned the miniature-painter, 'and he hasn't found me yet.'

'Extend the time,' said Hetty. 'This is a big town. Think of how many girls he might have to see soaked in water with their hair down before he would recognise you. The stew's getting on fine – but, oh, for an onion! I'd even use a piece of garlic, if I had it.'

The beef and potatoes bubbled merrily, exhaling a mouth-watering savour that yet lacked something leaving a hunger on the palate, a haunting, wistful desire for some lost and needful ingredient.

'I came near drowning in that awful river,' said Cecilia, shuddering.

'It ought to have more water in it,' said Hetty; 'the stew, I mean. I'll go get some at the sink.'

'It smells good,' said the artist.

'That nasty old North River?' objected Hetty. 'It smells to

me like soap factories and wet setter-dogs – oh, you mean the stew. Well, I wish we had an onion for it. Did he look like he had money?'

'First he looked kind,' said Cecilia. 'I'm sure he was rich; but that matters so little. When he drew out his bill-folder to pay the cabman you couldn't help seeing hundreds and thousands of dollars in it. And I looked over the cab doors and saw him leave the ferry station in a motor car; and the chauffeur gave him his bearskin to put on, for he was sopping wet. And it was only three days ago.'

'What a fool!' said Hetty shortly.

'Oh, the chauffeur wasn't wet,' breathed Cecilia. 'And he drove the car away very nicely.'

'I mean you,' said Hetty. 'For not giving him your address.'

'I never give my address to chauffeurs,' said Cecilia, haughtily.

'I wish we had one,' said Hetty, disconsolately.

'What for?'

'For the stew, of course – oh, I mean an onion.'

Hetty took a pitcher and started to the sink at the end of the hall.

A young man came down the steps from above just as she was opposite the lower step. He was decently dressed, but pale and haggard. His eyes were dull with the stress of some burden of physical or mental woe. In his hand he bore an onion – a pink, smooth, solid, shining onion, as large around as a ninety-eight-cent alarm clock.

Hetty stopped. So did the young man. There was something Joan of Arc-ish, Herculean, and Una-ish in the look and pose of the shop-lady – she had cast off the roles of Job and Little Red Riding Hood. The young man stopped at the foot of the stairs and coughed distractedly. He felt marooned, held up, attacked, assailed, levied upon, sacked, assessed, pan-handled, browbeaten, though he knew not why. It was the look in Hetty's eyes that did it. In them he saw the Jolly Roger fly to the masthead and an able seaman with a dirk between his teeth scurry up the ratlines and nail it there. But as yet he did not know that the cargo he carried was the thing that had caused him to be so nearly blown out of the water without even a parley.

'*Beg* your pardon,' said Hetty, as sweetly as her dilute acetic acid tones permitted, 'but did you find that onion on the stairs? There was a hole in the paper bag; and I've just come out to look for it.'

The young man coughed for half a minute. The interval may have given him the courage to defend his own property. Also, he clutched his pungent prize greedily, and, with a show of spirit, faced his grim waylayer.

'No,' he said huskily, 'I didn't find it on the stairs. It was given to me by Jack Bevens, on the top floor. If you don't believe it, ask him. I'll wait until you do.'

'I know about Bevens,' said Hetty, sourly. 'He writes books and things up there for the paper-and-rags man. We can hear the postman guy him all over the house when he brings them thick envelopes back. Say – do you live in the Vallambrosa?'

'I do not,' said the young man. 'I come to see Bevens sometimes. He's my friend. I live two blocks west.'

'What are you going to do with the onion? – *begging* your pardon,' said Hetty.

'I'm going to eat it.'

'Raw?'

'Yes: as soon as I get home.'

'Haven't you got anything else to eat with it?'

The young man considered briefly.

'No,' he confessed; 'there's not another scrap of anything in my diggings to eat. I think old Jack is pretty hard up for grub in his shack, too. He hated to give up the onion, but I worried him into parting with it.'

'Man,' said Hetty, fixing him with her world-sapient eyes, and laying a bony but impressive finger on his sleeve, 'you've known trouble, too, haven't you?'

'Lots,' said the onion owner, promptly. 'But this onion is my own property, honestly come by. If you will excuse me, I must be going.'

'Listen,' said Hetty, paling a little with anxiety. 'Raw onion is a mighty poor diet. And so is a beef-steak without one. Now, if you're Jack Bevens' friend, I guess you're nearly right. There's a little lady – a friend of mine – in my room there at the end of the hall. Both of us are out of luck; and we had just potatoes and meat between us. They're stewing now. But it ain't got any soul. There's something lacking to it. There's certain things in life that are naturally intended to fit and belong together. One is pink cheesecloth and green roses, and one is ham and eggs, and one is Irish and trouble. And the other one is beef and potatoes *with* onions. And still another one is people who are up against it and other people in the same fix.'

The young man went into a protracted paroxysm of coughing. With one hand he hugged his onion to his bosom.

'No doubt; no doubt,' said he, at length. 'But, as I said, I must be going because—'

Hetty clutched his sleeve firmly.

'Don't be a Dago, Little Brother. Don't eat raw onions. Chip it in toward the dinner and line yourself inside with the best stew you ever licked a spoon over. Must two ladies knock a young gentleman down and drag him inside for the honour of dining with 'em? No harm shall befall you, Little Brother. Loosen up and fall into line.'

The young man's pale face relaxed into a grim.

'Believe I'll go with you,' he said, brightening. 'If my onion is good as a credential, I'll accept the invitation gladly.'

'It's good as that, but better as seasoning,' said Hetty. 'You come and stand outside the door till I ask my lady friend if she has any objections. And don't run away with that letter of recommendation before I come out.'

Hetty went into her room and closed the door. The young man waited outside.

'Cecilia, kid,' said the shop-girl, oiling the sharp saw of her voice as well as she could, 'there's an onion outside. With a young man attached. I've asked him in to dinner. You ain't going to kick, are you?'

'Oh, dear!' said Cecilia, sitting up and patting her artistic hair. She cast a mournful glance at the ferry-boat poster on the wall.

'Nit,' said Hetty. 'It ain't him. You're up against real life now. I believe you said your hero friend had money and automobiles. This is a poor skeezicks that's got nothing to eat but an onion. But he's easy spoken and not a freshy. I imagine he's been a gentleman, he's so low down now. And we need the onion. Shall I bring him in? I'll guarantee his behaviour.'

'Hetty, dear,' sighed Cecilia, 'I'm so hungry. What difference does it make whether he's a prince or a burglar? I don't care. Bring him in if he's got anything to eat with him.'

Hetty went back into the hall. The onion man was gone. Her heart missed a beat, and a gray look settled over her face except her nose and cheekbones. And then the times of life flowed in again, for she saw him leaning out of the front window at the other end of the hall. She hurried there. He was shouting to someone below. The noise of the street over-powered the sound of her footsteps. She looked down over his shoulder, saw whom he was speaking to, and heard his words. He pulled himself in from the windowsill and saw her standing over him.

Hetty's eyes bored into him like two steel gimlets.

'Don't lie to me,' she said, calmly. 'What were you going to do with that onion?'

The young man suppressed a cough and faced her resolutely. His manner was that of one who had been bearded sufficiently.

'I was going to eat it,' said he, with emphatic slowness; 'just as I told you before.'

'And you have nothing else to eat at home?'

'Not a thing.'

'What kind of work do you do?'

'I am not working at anything just now.'

'Then why,' said Hetty, with her voice set on its sharpest edge, 'do you lean out of windows and give orders to chauffeurs in green automobiles in the street below?'

The young man flushed, and his dull eyes began to sparkle.

'Because, madam,' said he, in *accelerando* tones, 'I pay the chauffeur's wages and I own the automobile – and also this onion – this onion, madam.'

He flourished the onion within an inch of Hetty's nose. The shop-lady did not retreat a hair's-breadth.

'Then why do you eat onions,' she said, with biting contempt, 'and nothing else?'

'I never said I did,' retorted the young man, heatedly. 'I said I had nothing else to eat where I live. I am not a delicatessen storekeeper.'

'Then why,' pursued Hetty, inflexibly, 'were you going to eat a raw onion?

'My mother,' said the young man, 'always made me eat one for a cold. Pardon my referring to a physical infirmity; but you have noticed that I have a very, very severe cold. I was going to eat the onion and go to bed. I wonder why I am standing here and apologising to you for it.'

'How did you catch this cold?' went on Hetty, suspiciously.

The young man seemed to have arrived at some extreme height of feeling. There were two modes of descent open to him – a burst of rage or a surrender to the ridiculous. He chose wisely; and the empty hall echoed his hoarse laughter.

'You're a dandy,' said he. 'And I don't blame you for being careful. I don't mind telling you. I got wet. I was on a North River ferry a few days ago when a girl jumped overboard. Of course, I—'

Hetty extended her hand, interrupting his story.

'Give me the onion,' she said.

The young man set his jaw a trifle harder.

'Give me the onion,' she repeated.

He grinned and laid it in her hand.

Then Hetty's infrequent, grim, melancholy smile showed itself. She took the young man's arm and pointed with her other hand to the door of her room.

'Little Brother,' she said, 'go in there. The little fool you fished out of the river is there waiting for you. Go on in. I'll give you three minutes before I come. Potatoes is in there, waiting. Go on in, Onions.'

After he had tapped at the door and entered Hetty began to peel and wash the onion at the sink. She gave a grey look at the grey roofs outside, and the smile on her face vanished by little jerks and twitches.

'But it's us,' she said, grimly, to herself, 'it's *us* that furnished the beef.'

The Memento

Miss Lynnette D'Armande turned her back on Broadway. This was but tit for tat, because Broadway had often done the same thing to Miss D'Armande. Still, the 'tats' seemed to have it, for the ex-leading lady of the 'Reaping the Whirlwind' Company had everything to ask of Broadway, while there was no vice versa.

So Miss Lynnette D'Armande turned the back of her chair to her window that overlooked Broadway, and sat down to stitch in time the lisle-thread heel of a black silk stocking. The tumult and glitter of the roaring Broadway beneath her window had no charm for her; what she greatly desired was the stifling air of a dressing room on that fairyland street and the roar of an audience gathered in that capricious quarter. In the meantime, those stockings must not be neglected. Silk does wear out so, but – after all, isn't it just the only goods there is?

The Hotel Thalia looks on Broadway as Marathon looks on the sea. It stands like a gloomy cliff above the whirlpool where the tides of two great thoroughfares clash. Here the player-bands gather at the end of their wanderings, to loosen the buskin and dust the sock. Thick in the streets around it are booking offices, theatres, agents, schools, and the lobster-palaces to which those thorny paths lead.

Wandering through the eccentric halls of the dim and fusty Thalia, you seem to have found yourself in some great ark or caravan about to sail, or fly, or roll away on wheels. About the house lingers a sense of unrest, of expectation, of transientness, even of anxiety and apprehension. The halls are a labyrinth. Without a guide you wander like a lost soul in a Sam Loyd puzzle.

Turning any corner, a dressing-sack or a *cul-de-sac* may bring you up short. You meet alarming tragedians stalking in bathrobes in search of rumoured bathrooms. From hundreds of rooms come the buzz of talk, scraps of new and old songs, and the ready laughter of the convened players.

Summer has come; their companies have disbanded, and they take their rest in their favourite caravansary, while they besiege the managers for engagements for the coming season.

At this hour of the afternoon the day's work of tramping the rounds of the agents' offices is over. Past you, as you ramble distractedly through the mossy halls, flit audible visions of houris, with veiled, starry eyes, flying tag-ends of things, and a swish of silk, bequeathing to the dull hallways an odour of gaiety and a memory of *frangipanni*. Serious young comedians, with versatile Adam's apples, gather in doorways and talk of Booth. Far-reaching from somewhere comes the smell of ham and red cabbage, and the crash of dishes on the American plan.

The indeterminate hum of life in the Thalia is enlivened by the discreet popping – at reasonable and salubrious intervals – of beer-bottle corks. Thus punctuated, life in the genial hostel scans easily – the comma being the favourite mark, semicolons frowned upon, and periods barred.

Miss D'Armande's room was a small one. There was room for her rocker between the dresser and the washstand if it were placed longitudinally. On the dresser were its usual accoutrements, plus the ex-leading lady's collected souvenirs of road engagements and photographs of her dearest and best professional friends.

At one of these photographs she looked twice or thrice as she darned, and smiled friendlily.

'I'd like to know where Lee is just this minute,' she said, half-aloud.

If you had been privileged to view the photograph thus flattered, you would have thought at the first glance that you saw the picture of a many-petalled, white flower, blown through the air by a storm. But the floral kingdom was not responsible for that swirl of petalous whiteness.

You saw the filmy, brief skirt of Miss Rosalie Ray as she made a complete heels-over-head turn in her wistaria-entwined swing, far out from the stage, high above the heads of the audience. You saw the camera's inadequate representation of the graceful, strong kick, with which she, at this exciting moment, sent flying, high and far, the yellow silk garter that each evening spun from her agile limb and descended upon the delighted audience below.

You saw, too, amid the black-clothed, mainly masculine patrons of select vaudeville a hundred hands raised with the hope of staying the flight of the brilliant aerial token.

Forty weeks of the best circuits this act had brought Miss Rosalie Ray for each of two years. She did other things during her twelve minutes – a song and dance, imitations of two or three actors who are but imitations of themselves, and a balancing feat with a stepladder and feather duster; but when the blossom-decked swing was let down from the flies, and Miss Rosalie sprang smiling into the seat, with the golden circlet conspicuous in the place whence it was soon to slide and become a soaring and coveted guerdon – then it was that the audience rose in its seat as a single man – or presumably so – and endorsed the speciality that made Miss Ray's name a favourite in the booking-offices.

At the end of the two years Miss Ray suddenly announced to her dear friend, Miss D'Armande, that she was going to spend the summer at an antediluvian village on the north shore of Long Island, and that the stage would see her no more. Seventeen minutes after Miss Lynnette D'Armande had expressed her wish to know the whereabouts of her old chum, there were sharp raps at her door.

Doubt not that it was Rosalie Ray. At the shrill command to enter she did so, with something of a tired flutter, and dropped a heavy handbag on the floor. Upon my word, it was Rosalie, in a loose, travel-stained automobileless coat, closely tied brown veil with yard-long flying ends, gray walking-suit and tan Oxfords with lavender over-gaiters.

When she threw off her veil and hat, you saw a pretty enough face, now flushed and disturbed by some unusual emotion, and restless, large eyes with discontent marring their brightness. A heavy pile of dull auburn hair, hastily put up, was escaping in crinkly waving strands and curling small locks from the confining combs and pins.

The meeting of the two was not marked by the effusion vocal, gymnastical, osculatory and catechetical that distinguishes the greetings of their unprofessional sisters in society. There was a brief clinch, two simultaneous labial dabs, and they stood on the same footing of the old days. Very much like the short salutations of soldiers or of travellers in foreign wilds are the welcomes between the strollers at the corners of their criss-cross roads.

'I've got the hall-room two flights up above yours,' said Rosalie, 'but I came straight to see you before going up. I didn't know you were here till they told me.'

'I've been in since the last of April,' said Lynnette. 'And I'm going on the road with a "Fatal Inheritance" Company. We open next week in Elizabath. I thought you'd quit the stage, Lee. Tell me about yourself.'

Rosalie settled herself with a skilful wriggle on the top of Miss D'Armande's wardrobe trunk, and leaned her head against the papered wall. From long habit, thus can peripatetic leading ladies and their sisters make themselves as comfortable as though the deepest armchairs embraced them.

'I'm going to tell you, Lynn,' she said, with a strangely sardonic and yet carelessly resigned look on her youthful face. 'And then tomorrow I'll strike the old Broadway trail again, and wear some more paint off the chairs in the agents' offices. If anybody had told me any time in the last three months up to four o'clock this afternoon that I'd ever listen to that "Leave-your-name-and-address" rot of the booking bunch again, I'd have given 'em the real Mrs Fiske laugh. Loan me a handkerchief, Lynn. Gee! but those Long Island trains are fierce. I've got enough soft coal cinders on my face to go on and play *Topsy* without using the cork. And, speaking of corks – got anything to drink, Lynn?'

Miss D'Armande opened a door of the washstand and took out a bottle.

'There's nearly a pint of Manhattan. There's a cluster of carnations in the drinking-glass, but—'

'Oh, pass the bottle. Save the glass for company. Thanks! That hits the spot. The same to you. My first drink in three months!'

'Yes, Lynn, I quit the stage at the end of last season. I quit it because I was sick of the life. And especially because my heart and soul were sick of men – of the kind of men we stage people have to be up against. You know what the game is to us – it's a fight against 'em all the way down the line, from the manager who wants us to try his new motor car to the bill-posters who want to call us by our front names.

'And the men we have to meet after the show are the worst of all. The stage-door kind, and the manager's friends who take us to supper, and show their diamonds, and talk about seeing "Dan" and "Dave" and "Charlie" for us. They're beasts, and I hate 'em.

'I tell you, Lynn, it's the girls like us on the stage that ought to be pitied. It's girls from good homes that are honestly ambitious and work hard to rise in the profession, but never do get there. You hear a lot of sympathy sloshed around on chorus girls and their fifteen dollars a week. Piffle! There ain't a sorrow in the chorus that a lobster cannot heal.

'If there's any tears to shed, let 'em fall for the actress that gets a salary of from thirty to forty-five dollars a week for taking a leading part in a bum show. She knows she'll never do any better; but she hangs on for years, hoping for the "chance" that never comes.

'And the fool plays we have to work in! Having another girl roll you around the stage by the hind legs in a "Wheelbarrow Chorus" in a musical comedy is dignified drama compared with the idiotic things I've had to do in the thirty-centres.

'But what I hated most was the men – the men leering and blathering at you across tables, trying to buy you with Würzburger or Extra Dry, according to their estimate of your price. And the men in the audiences, clapping, yelling, snarling, crowding, writhing, gloating – like a lot of wild beasts, with their eyes fixed on you, ready to eat you up if you come in reach of their claws. Oh, how I hate 'em!

'Well, I'm not telling you much about myself, am I, Lynn?

'I had two hundred dollars saved up, and I cut the stage the first of the summer. I went over on Long Island, and found the sweetest little village that ever was, called Soundport, right on the water. I was going to spend the summer there, and study up on elocution, and try to get a class in the fall. There was an old widow lady with a cottage near the beach who sometimes rented a room or two just for company, and she took me in. She had another boarder, too – the Reverend Arthur Lyle.

'Yes, he was the headliner. You're on, Lynn. I'll tell you all of it in a minute. It's only a one-act play.

'The first time he walked on, Lynn, I felt myself going; the first lines he spoke, he had me. He was different from the men in audiences. He was tall and slim, and you never heard him come in the room, but you *felt* him. He had a face like a picture of a knight – like one of that Round Table bunch – and a voice like a 'cello solo. And his manners!

'Lynn, if you'd take John Drew in his best drawing-room scene and compare the two you'd have John arrested for disturbing the peace.

'I'll spare you the particulars; but in less than a month Arthur and I were engaged. He preached at a little one-night stand of a Methodist church. There was to be a parsonage the size of a lunch-wagon, and hens and honeysuckles when we were married. Arthur used to preach to me a good deal about Heaven, but he never could get my mind quite off those honeysuckles and hens.

'No; I didn't tell him I'd been on the stage. I hated the business and all that went with it; I'd cut it out for ever, and I didn't see any use of stirring things up. I was a good girl, and I didn't have anything to confess, except being an elocutionist, and that was about all the strain my conscience would stand.

'Oh, I tell you, Lynn, I was happy. I sang in the choir and attended the sewing society, and recited that "Annie Laurie" thing with the whistling stunt in it, "in a manner bordering upon the professional," as the weekly village paper reported it. And Arthur and I went rowing, and walking in the woods, and clamming, and that poky little village seemed to me the best place in the world. I'd have been happy to live there always, too, if—

'But one morning old Mrs Gurley, the widow lady, got gossipy while I was helping her string beans on the back porch, and began to gush information, as folks who rent out their rooms usually do. Mr Lyle was her idea of a saint on earth – as he was mine, too. She went over all his virtues and graces, and wound up by telling me that Arthur had had an extremely romantic love-affair, not long before, that had ended unhappily. She didn't seem to be on to the details, but she knew that he had been hit pretty hard. He was paler and thinner, she said, and he had some kind of a remembrance or keepsake of the lady in a little rosewood box that he kept locked in his desk drawer in his study.

' "Several times," says she, "I've seen him gloomerin' over that box of evenings, and he always locks it up right away if anybody comes into the room."

'Well, you can imagine how long it was before I got Arthur by the wrist and led him down stage and hissed in his ear.

'That same afternoon we were lazying around in a boat among the water lilies at the edge of the bay.

' "Arthur," says I, "you never told me you'd had another love affair. But Mrs Gurley did," I went on, to let him know I knew. I hate to hear a man lie.

'"Before you came," says he, looking me frankly in the eye, "there was a previous affection – a strong one. Since you know of it, I will be perfectly candid with you."

' "I am waiting," says I.

' "My dear Ida," says Arthur – of course, I went by my real name while I was in Soundport – "this former affection was a spiritual one, in fact. Although the lady aroused my deepest sentiments, and was, as I thought, my ideal woman, I never met her, and never spoke to her. It was an ideal love. My love for you, while no less ideal, is different. You wouldn't let that come between us."

' "Was she pretty?" I asked.

' "She was very beautiful," said Arthur.

' "Did you see her often?" I asked.

' "Something like a dozen times," says he

' "Always from a distance?" says I.

' "Always from quite a distance," says he.

' "And you loved her?" I asked.

' "She seemed my ideal of beauty and grace – and soul," says Arthur.

' "And this keepsake that you keep under lock and key, and moon over at times, is that a remembrance from her?"

' "A memento," says Arthur, "that I have treasured."

' "Did she send it to you?"

' "It came to me from her," says he.

' "In a roundabout way?" I asked.

' "Somewhat roundabout," says he, "and yet rather direct."

' "Why didn't you ever meet her?" I asked. "Were your positions in life so different?"

' "She was far above me," says Arthur. "Now, Ida," he goes on, "this is all of the past. You're not going to be jealous, are you?"

' "Jealous!" says I. "Why, man, what are you talking about? It makes me think ten times as much of you as I did before I knew about it."

'And it did, Lynn – if you can understand it. That ideal

love was a new one on me, but it struck me as being the most beautiful and glorious thing I'd ever heard of. Think of a man loving a woman he'd never even spoken to, and being faithful just to what his mind and heart pictured her. Oh, it sounded great to me. The men I'd always known come at you with either diamonds, knock-out-drops or a raise of salary – and their ideals! – well, we'll say no more.

'Yes, it made me think more of Arthur than I did before. I couldn't be jealous of that faraway divinity that he used to worship, for I was going to have him myself. And I began to look upon him as a saint on earth, just as old lady Gurley did.

'About four o'clock this afternoon a man came to the house for Arthur to go and see somebody that was sick among his church bunch. Old lady Gurley was taking her afternoon snore on a couch, so that left me pretty much alone.

'In passing by Arthur's study I looked in, and saw his bunch of keys hanging in the drawer of his desk, where he'd forgotten 'em. Well, I guess we're all to the Mrs Bluebeard now and then, ain't we, Lynn? I made up my mind I'd have a look at that memento he kept so secret. Not that I cared where it was – it was just curiosity.

'While I was opening the drawer I imagined one or two things it might be. I thought it might be a dried rosebud she'd dropped down to him from a balcony, or maybe a picture of her he'd cut out of a magazine, she being so high up in the world.

'I opened the drawer, and there was the rosewood casket about the size of a gent's collar box I found the little key in the bunch that fitted it and unlocked it and raised the lid.

'I took one look at that memento, and then I went to my room and packed my trunk. I threw a few things into my grip, gave my hair a flirt or two with a side-comb, put on my hat, and went in and gave the old lady's foot a kick. I'd tried awfully hard to use proper and correct language while I was there for Arthur's sake, and I had the habit down pat, but it left me then.

' "Stop sawing gourds," says I, "and sit up and take notice. The ghost's about to walk. I'm going away from here, and I owe you eight dollars. The express man will call for my trunk."

'I handed her the money.

' "Dear me, Miss Crosby!" says she. "Is anything wrong? I thought you were pleased here. Dear me, young women are so hard to understand, and so different from what you expect 'em to be."

' "You're damn right," says I. "Some of 'em are. But you can't say that about men. *When you know one man you know 'em all!* That settles the human-race question."

'And then I caught the four-thirty-eight, soft-coal unlimited; and here I am.'

'You didn't tell me what was in the box, Lee,' said Miss D'Armande anxiously.

'One of those yellow silk garters that I used to kick off my leg into the audience during that old vaudeville swing act of mine. Is there any of the cocktail left, Lynn!'

The Furnished Room

Restless, shifting, fugacious as time itself, is a certain vast bulk of the population of the redbrick district of the Lower West Side. Homeless, they have a hundred homes. They flit from furnished room to furnished room, transients for ever – transients in abode, transients in heart and mind. They sing 'Home Sweet Home' in ragtime; they carry their *lares et penates* in a bandbox; their vine is entwined about a picture hat; a rubber plant is their fig tree.

Hence the houses of this district, having had a thousand dwellers, should have a thousand tales to tell, mostly dull ones, no doubt; but it would be strange if there could not be found a ghost or two in the wake of all these vagrant ghosts.

One evening after dark a young man prowled among these crumbling red mansions, ringing their bells. At the twelfth he rested his lean hand-baggage upon the step and wiped the dust from his hatband and forehead. The bell sounded faint and far away in some remote, hollow depths.

To the door of this, the twelfth house whose bell he had rung, came a housekeeper who made him think of an unwholesome, surfeited worm that had eaten its nut to a hollow shell and now sought to fill the vacancy with edible lodgers.

He asked if there was a room to let.

'Come in,' said the housekeeper. Her voice came from her throat; her throat seemed lined with fur. 'I have the third floor back, vacant since a week back. Should you wish to look at it?'

The young man followed her up the stairs. A faint light from no particular source mitigated the shadows of the halls. They trod noiselessly upon a stair carpet that its own loom would have forsworn. It seemed to have become vegetable; to have degenerated in that rank, sunless air to lush lichen or spreading moss that grew in patches to the staircase and was viscid under the foot like organic matter. At each turn of the stairs were vacant niches in the wall. Perhaps plants had once been set within them. If so they had died in that foul and tainted air. It may be that statues of the saints had stood there, but it was not difficult to conceive that imps and devils had dragged them forth in the darkness and down to the unholy depths of some furnished pit below.

'This is the room,' said the housekeeper, from her furry throat. 'It's a nice room. It ain't often vacant. I had some most elegant people in it last summer – no trouble at all, and paid in advance to the minute. The water's at the end of the hall. Sprowls and Mooney – kept it three months. They done a vaudeville sketch. Miss B'retta Sprowls – you may have heard of her – Oh, that was just the stage names – right there over the dresser is where the marriage certificate hung, framed. The gas is here, and you see there is plenty of closet room. It's a room everybody likes. It never stays idle long.'

'Do you have many theatrical people rooming here?' asked the young man.

'They comes and goes. A good proportion of my lodgers is connected with the theatres. Yes, sir, this is the theatrical district. Actor people never stays long anywhere. I get my share. Yes, they comes and they goes.'

He engaged the room, paying for a week in advance. He was tired, he said, and would take possession at once. He counted out the money. The room had been made ready, she said, even to towels and water. As the housekeeper moved away he put, for the thousandth time, the question that he carried at the end of his tongue.

'A young girl – Miss Vashner – Miss Eloise Vashner – do you remember such a one among your lodgers? She would be singing on the stage, most likely. A fair girl, of medium height and slender, with reddish gold hair and a dark mole near her left eyebrow.'

'No, I don't remember the name. Them stage people has names they change as often as their rooms. They comes and they goes. No, I don't call that one to mind.'

No. Always no. Five months of ceaseless interrogation and the inevitable negative. So much time spent by day in questioning managers, agents, schools and choruses; by night among the audiences of theatres from all-star casts down to music halls so low that he dreaded to find what he most hoped for. He who had loved her best had tried to find her. He was sure that since her disappearance from home this great water-girt city held her somewhere, but it was like a monstrous quicksand, shifting its particles constantly, with no foundation, its upper granules of today buried tomorrow in ooze and slime.

The furnished room received its latest guest with a first glow of pseudo-hospitality, a hectic, haggard, perfunctory welcome like the specious smile of a demi-rep. The sophistical comfort came in reflected gleams from the decayed furniture, the ragged brocade upholstery of a couch and two chairs, a footwide cheap pier-glass between the two windows, from one or two gilt picture frames and a brass bedstead in a corner.

The guest reclined, inert, upon a chair, while the room, confused in speech as though it were an apartment in Babel, tried to discourse to him of its divers tenantry.

A polychromatic rug like some brilliant-flowered, rectangular, tropical islet lay surrounded by a billowy sea of soiled matting. Upon the gay-papered wall were those pictures that pursue the homeless one from house to house – The Huguenot Lovers, The First Quarrel, The Wedding Breakfast, Psyche at the Fountain. The mantel's chastely severe outline was ingloriously veiled behind some pert drapery drawn rakishly askew like the sashes of the Amazonian ballet. Upon it was some desolate flotsam cast aside by the room's marooned when a lucky sail had borne them to a fresh port – a trifling vase or two, pictures of actresses, a medicine bottle, some stray cards out of a deck.

One by one, as the characters of a cryptograph become explicit, the little signs left by the furnished room's procession of guests developed a significance. The threadbare space in the rug in front of the dresser told that lovely woman had marched in the throng. Tiny fingerprints on the wall spoke of little prisoners trying to feel their way to sun and air. A splattered stain, raying like the shadow of a bursting bomb, witnessed where a hurled glass or bottle had splintered with its contents against the wall. Across the pier-glass had been scrawled with a diamond in staggering letters the name 'Marie'. It seemed that the succession of dwellers in the furnished room had turned in fury – perhaps tempted beyond forbearance by its garish coldness – and wreaked upon it their passions. The furniture was chipped and bruised; the couch, distorted by bursting springs, seemed a horrible monster that had been slain during the stress of some grotesque convulsion. Some more potent upheaval had cloven a great slice from the marble mantel. Each plank in the floor owned its particular cant and shriek as from a separate and individual agony. It seemed incredible that all this malice and injury had been wrought upon the room by those who had called it for a time their home; and yet it may have been the cheated home instinct surviving blindly, the resentful rage at false household gods that had kindled their wrath. A hut that is our own we can sweep and adorn and cherish.

The young tenant in the chair allowed these thoughts to file, soft-shod, through his mind, while there drifted into the room furnished sounds and furnished scents. He heard in one room a tittering and incontinent, slack laughter; in others the monologue of a scold, the rattling of dice, a lullaby, and one crying dully; above him a banjo tinkled with spirit. Doors banged somewhere; the elevated trains roared intermittently; a cat yowled miserably upon a back fence. And he breathed the breath of the house – a dank savour rather than a smell – a cold, musty effluvium as from underground vaults mingled with the reeking exhalations of linoleum and mildewed and rotten woodwork.

Then, suddenly, as he rested there, the room was filled with the strong, sweet odour of mignonette. It came as upon a single buffet of wind with such sureness and fragrance and emphasis that it almost seemed a living visitant. And the man cried aloud, 'What, dear?' as if he had been called, and sprang up and faced about. The rich odour clung to him and wrapped him about. He reached out his arms for it, all his senses for the time confused and commingled. How could one be peremptorily called by an odour? Surely it must have been a sound. But, was it not the sound that had touched, that had caressed him?

'She has been in this room,' he cried, and he sprang to wrest from it a token, for he knew he would recognise the smallest thing that had belonged to her or that she had touched. This enveloping scent of mignonette, the odour that she had loved and made her own – whence came it?

The room had been but carelessly set in order. Scattered upon the flimsy dresser scarf were half a dozen hairpins – those discreet, indistinguishable friends of womankind, feminine of gender, infinite of mood and uncommunicative of tense. These he ignored, conscious of their triumphant lack of identity. Ransacking the drawers of the dresser he came upon a discarded, tiny, ragged handkerchief. He pressed it to his face. It was racy and insolent with heliotrope; he hurled it to the floor. In another drawer he found odd buttons, a theatre programme, a pawnbroker's card, two lost marshmallows, a book on the divination of dreams. In the last was a woman's black satin hair-bow, which halted him, poised between ice and fire. But the black satin hair-bow also is femininity's demure, impersonal, common ornament, and tells no tales.

And then he traversed the room like a hound on the scent, skimming the walls, considering the corners of the bulging matting on his hands and knees, rummaging mantel and tables, the curtains and hangings, the drunken cabinet in the corner, for a visible sign unable to perceive that she was there beside, around, against, within, above him, clinging to him, wooing him, calling him so poignantly through the finer senses that even his grosser ones became cognisant of the call. Once again he answered loudly, 'Yes, dear!' and turned, wild-eyed, to gaze on vacancy, for he could not yet discern form and colour and love and outstretched arms in the odour of mignonette. Oh, God! whence that odour, and since when have odours had a voice to call? Thus he groped.

He burrowed in crevices and corners, and found corks and cigarettes. These he passed in passive contempt. But once he found in a fold of the matting a half-smoked cigar, and this he ground beneath his heel with a green and trenchant oath.

He sifted the room from end to end. He found dreary and ignoble small records of many a peripatetic tenant; but of her whom he sought, and who may have lodged there, and whose spirit seemed to hover there, he found no trace.

And then he thought of the housekeeper.

He ran from the haunted room downstairs and to a door that showed a crack of light. She came out to his knock. He smothered his excitement as best he could.

'Will you tell me, madam,' he besought her, 'who occupied the room I have before I came?'

'Yes, sir. I can tell you again. 'Twas Sprowls and Mooney, as I said. Miss B'retta Sprowls it was in the theatres, but Mrs Mooney she was. My house is well known for respectability. The marriage certificate hung, framed, on a nail over – '

'What kind of a lady was Miss Sprowls – in looks, I mean?'

'Why, black-haired, sir, short and stout, with a comical face. They left a week ago Tuesday.'

'And before they occupied it?'

'Why, there was a single gentleman connected with the draying business. He left owing me a week. Before him was Mrs Crowder and her two children, that stayed four months; and back of them was old Mr Doyle, whose sons paid for him. He kept the room six months. That goes back a year, sir, and further I do not remember.'

He thanked her and crept back to his room. The room was dead. The essence that had vivified it was gone. The perfume of mignonette had departed. In its place was the old, stale odour of mouldy house furniture, of atmosphere in storage.

The ebbing of his hope drained his faith. He sat staring at the yellow, singing gaslight. Soon he walked to the bed and began to tear the sheets into strips. With the blade of his knife he drove them tightly into every crevice around windows and door. When all was snug and taut he turned out the light turned the gas full on again and laid himself gratefully upon the bed.

*   *   *

It was Mrs McCool's night to go with the can for beer. So she fetched it and sat with Mrs Purdy in one of those subterranean retreats where housekeepers foregather and the worm dieth seldom.

'I rented out my third floor back, this evening,' said Mrs Purdy, across a fine circle of foam. 'A young man took it. He went up to bed two hours ago.'

'Now, did ye, Mrs Purdy, ma'am?' said Mrs McCool, with intense admiration. 'You do be a wonder for rentin' rooms of that kind. And did ye tell him, then?' she concluded in a husky whisper, laden with mystery.

'Rooms,' said Mrs Purdy, in her furriest tones, 'are furnished for to rent. I did not tell him, Mrs McCool.'

' 'Tis right ye are, ma'am; 'tis by renting rooms we kape alive. Ye have the rale sense for business, ma'am. There be many people will rayjict the rentin' of a room if they be tould a suicide has been after dyin' in the bed of it.'

'As you say, we has our living to be making,' remarked Mrs Purdy.

'Yis, ma'am; 'tis true. 'Tis just one wake ago this day I helped ye lay out the third floor back. A pretty slip of a colleen she was to be killin' herself wid the gas a swate little face she had, Mrs Purdy, ma'am.'

'She'd a-been called handsome, as you say,' said Mrs Purdy, assenting but critical, 'but for that mole she had a-growin' by her left eyebrow. Do fill up your glass again, Mrs McCool.'

The Last Leaf

In a little district west of Washington Square the streets have run crazy and broken themselves into small strips called 'places'. These 'places' make strange angles and curves. One street crosses itself a time or two. An artist once discovered a valuable possibility in this street. Suppose a collector with a bill for paints, paper and canvas should, in traversing this route, suddenly meet himself coming back, without a cent having been paid on account!

So, to quaint old Greenwich Village the art people soon came prowling, hunting for north windows and eighteenth-century gables and Dutch attics and low rents. Then they imported some pewter mugs and a chafing dish or two from Sixth Avenue, and became a 'colony'.

At the top of a squatty, three-storey brick Sue and Johnsy had their studio. 'Johnsy' was familiar for Joanna. One was from Maine, the other from California. They had met at the *table d'hôte* of an Eighth Street 'Delmonico's', and found their tastes in art, chicory salad and bishop sleeves so congenial that the joint studio resulted.

That was in May. In November a cold, unseen stranger, whom the doctors called Pneumonia, stalked about the colony, touching one here and there with his icy finger. Over on the East Side this ravager strode boldly, smiting his victims by scores, but his feet trod slowly through the maze of the narrow and moss-grown 'places'.

Mr Pneumonia was not what you would call a chivalric old

gentleman. A mite of a little woman with blood thinned by Californian zephyrs was hardly fair game for the red-fisted, short-breathed old duffer. But Johnsy he smote; and she lay, scarcely moving, on her painted iron bedstead, looking through the small Dutch windowpanes at the blank side of the next brick house.

One morning the busy doctor invited Sue into the hallway with a shaggy, grey eyebrow.

'She has one chance in – let us say, ten,' he said, as he shook down the mercury in his clinical thermometer. 'And that chance is for her to want to live. This way people have of lining up on the side of the undertaker makes the entire pharmacopoeia look silly. Your little lady has made up her mind that she's not going to get well. Has she anything on her mind?'

'She – she wanted to paint the Bay of Naples some day,' said Sue.

'Paint? – bosh! Has she anything on her mind worth thinking about twice – a man, for instance?'

'A man?' said Sue, with a jews'-harp twang in her voice. 'Is a man worth – but, no, doctor; there is nothing of the kind.'

'Well, it is the weakness, then,' said the doctor. 'I will do all that science, so far as it may filter through my efforts, can accomplish. But whenever my patient begins to count the carriages in her funeral procession I subtract fifty per cent from the curative power of medicines. If you will get her to ask one question about the new winter styles in cloak sleeves I will promise you a one-in-five chance for her, instead of one in ten.'

After the doctor had gone, Sue went into the workroom and cried a Japanese napkin to a pulp. Then she swaggered into Johnsy's room with her drawing-board, whistling ragtime.

Johnsy lay, scarcely making a ripple under the bedclothes,

with her face toward the window. Sue stopped whistling, thinking she was asleep.

She arranged her board and began a pen-and-ink drawing to illustrate a magazine story. Young artists must pave their way to Art by drawing pictures for magazine stories that young authors write to pave their way to Literature.

As Sue was sketching a pair of elegant horseshow riding trousers and a monocle on the figure of the hero, an Idaho cowboy, she heard a low sound, several times repeated. She went quickly to the bedside.

Johnsy's eyes were open wide. She was looking out the window and counting – counting backward.

'Twelve,' she said, and a little later, 'eleven'; and then 'ten', and 'nine'; and then 'eight' and 'seven', almost together.

Sue looked solicitously out the window. What was there to count? There was only a bare, dreary yard to be seen, and the blank side of the brick house twenty feet away. An old, old ivy vine, gnarled and decayed at the roots, climbed halfway up the brick wall. The cold breath of autumn had stricken its leaves from the vine until its skeleton branches clung, almost bare, to the crumbling bricks.

'What is it, dear?' asked Sue.

'Six,' said Johnsy, in almost a whisper. 'They're falling faster now. Three days ago there were almost a hundred. It made my head ache to count them. But now it's easy. There goes another one. There are only five left now.'

'Five what, dear? Tell your Sudie.'

'Leaves. On the ivy vine. When the last one falls I must go too. I've known that for three days. Didn't the doctor tell you?'

'Oh, I never heard of such nonsense,' complained Sue, with magnificent scorn. 'What have old ivy leaves to do with your getting well? And you used to love that vine so, you naughty girl. Don't be a goosey. Why, the doctor told me this morning that your chances for getting well real soon were – let's see exactly what he said – he said the chances were ten to one! Why, that's almost as good a chance as we have in New York when we ride on the streetcars or walk past a new building. Try to take some broth now, and let Sudie go back to her drawing, so she can sell the editor man with it, and buy port wine for her sick child, and pork chops for her greedy self.'

'You needn't get any more wine,' said Johnsy, keeping her eyes fixed out the window.

'There goes another. No, I don't want any broth. That leaves just four. I want to see the last one fall before it gets dark. Then I'll go too.'

'Johnsy, dear,' said Sue, bending over her, 'will you promise me to keep your eyes closed, and not look out of the window until I am done working? I must hand those drawings in by tomorrow. I need the light or I would draw the shade down.'

'Couldn't you draw in the other room?' asked Johnsy coldly.

'I'd rather be here by you,' said Sue. 'Besides, I don't want you to keep looking at those silly ivy leaves.'

'Tell me as soon as you have finished,' said Johnsy, closing her eyes, and lying white and still as a fallen statue, 'because I want to see the last one fall. I'm tired of waiting. I'm tired of thinking. I want to turn loose my hold on everything, and go sailing down, down, just like one of those poor, tired leaves.'

'Try to sleep,' said Sue. 'I must call Behrman up to be my model for the old hermit miner. I'll not be gone a minute. Don't try to move till I come back.'

Old Behrman was a painter who lived on the ground floor beneath them. He was past sixty and had a Michelangelo's Moses beard curling down from the head of a satyr along the body of an imp. Behrman was a failure in art. Forty years he had wielded the brush without getting near enough to touch the hem of his Mistress's robe. He had been always about to paint a masterpiece, but had never yet begun it. For several years he had painted nothing except now and then a daub in the line of commerce or advertising. He earned a little by serving as a model to those young artists in the colony who could not pay the price of a professional. He drank gin to excess, and still talked of his coming masterpiece. For the rest he was a fierce little old man, who scoffed terribly at softness in anyone, and who regarded himself as especial mastiff-in-waiting to protect the two young artists in the studio above.

Sue found Behrman smelling strongly of juniper berries in his dimly-lighted den below. In one corner was a blank canvas on an easel that had been waiting there for twenty-five years to receive the first line of the masterpiece. She told him of Johnsy's fancy, and how she feared she would, indeed, light and fragile as a leaf herself, float away when her slight hold upon the world grew weaker.

Old Behrman, with his red eyes plainly streaming, shouted his contempt and derision for such idiotic imaginings.

'Vass!' he cried. 'Is dere people in de world mit der foolishness to die because leafs dey drop off from a confounded vine? I haf not heard of such a thing. No, I vill not bose as a model for your fool hermit-dunderhead. Vy do you allow dot silly pusiness to come in der prain of her? Ach, dot poor little Miss Yohnsy.'

'She is very ill and weak,' said Sue, 'and the fever has left her mind morbid and full of strange fancies. Very well, Mr Behrman, if you do not care to pose for me, you needn't. But I think you are a horrid old – old flibbertigibbet.'

'You are just like a woman!' yelled Behrman. 'Who said I

vill not bose? Go on. I come mit you. For half an hour I haf peen trying to say dot I am ready to bose. Gott! dis is not any blace in which one so goot as Miss Yohnsy shall lie sick. Some day I vill baint a masterpiece, and ve shall all go avay. Gott! yes.'

Johnsy was sleeping when they went upstairs. Sue pulled the shade down to the window-sill and motioned Behrman into the other room. In there they peered out the window fearfully at the ivy vine. Then they looked at each other for a moment without speaking. A persistent, cold rain was falling, mingled with snow. Behrman, in his old blue shirt, took his seat as the hermit-miner on an upturned kettle for a rock.

When Sue awoke from an hour's sleep the next morning she found Johnsy with dull, wide-open eyes staring at the drawn green shade.

'Pull it up! I want to see,' she ordered, in a whisper.

Wearily Sue obeyed.

But, lo! after the beating rain and fierce gusts of wind that had endured through the livelong night, there yet stood out against the brick wall one ivy leaf. It was the last on the vine. Still dark green near its stem, but with its serrated edges tinted with the yellow of dissolution and decay, it hung bravely from a branch some twenty feet above the ground.

'It is the last one,' said Johnsy. 'I thought it would surely fall during the night. I heard the wind. It will fall today, and I shall die at the same time.'

'Dear, dear!' said Sue, leaning her worn face down to the pillow; 'think of me, if you won't think of yourself. What would I do?'

But Johnsy did not answer. The lonesomest thing in all the world is a soul when it is making ready to go on its mysterious, far journey. The fancy seemed to possess her more strongly as one by one the ties that bound her to friendship and to earth were loosed.

The day wore away, and even through the twilight they could see the lone ivy leaf clinging to its stem against the wall. And then, with the coming of the night the north wind was again loosed, while the rain still beat against the windows and pattered down from the low Dutch eaves.

When it was light enough Johnsy, the merciless, commanded that the shade be raised.

The ivy leaf was still there.

Johnsy lay for a long time looking at it. And then she called to Sue, who was stirring her chicken broth over the gas stove.

'I've been a bad girl, Sudie,' said Johnsy. 'Something has made that last leaf stay there to show me how wicked I was. It is a sin to want to die. You may bring me a little broth now, and some milk with a little port in it, and – no; bring me a hand-mirror first; and then pack some pillows about me, and I will sit up and watch you cook.'

An hour later she said – 'Sudie, some day I hope to paint the Bay of Naples.'

The doctor came in the afternoon, and Sue had an excuse to go into the hallway as he left.

'Even chances,' said the doctor, talking Sue's thin, shaking hand in his. 'With good nursing you'll win. And now I must see another case I have downstairs. Behrman, his name is – some kind of an artist, I believe. Pneumonia, too. He is an old, weak man, and the attack is acute. There is no hope for him; but he goes to the hospital today to be made more comfortable.'

The next day the doctor said to Sue: 'She's out of danger. You've won. Nutrition and care now – that's all.'

And that afternoon Sue came to the bed where Johnsy lay,

contentedly knitting a very blue and very useless woollen shoulder scarf, and put one arm around her, pillows and all.

'I have something to tell you, white mouse,' she said. 'Mr Behrman died of pneumonia today in hospital. He was ill only two days. The janitor found him on the morning of the first day in his room downstairs helpless with pain. His shoes and clothing were wet through and icy cold. They couldn't imagine where he had been on such a dreadful night. And then they found a lantern, still lighted, and a ladder that had been dragged from its place, and some scattered brushes, and a palette with green and yellow colours mixed on it, and – look out the window, dear, at the last ivy leaf on the wall. Didn't you wonder why it never fluttered or moved when the wind blew? Ah, darling, it's Behrman's masterpiece – he painted it there the night that the last leaf fell.'

The Trimmed Lamp

Of course there are two sides to the question. Let us look at the other. We often hear 'shop-girls' spoken of. No such persons exist. There are girls who work in shops. They make their living that way. But why turn their occupation into an adjective? Let us be fair. We do not refer to the girls who live on Fifth Avenue as 'marriage-girls'.

Lou and Nancy were chums. They came to the big city to find work because there was not enough to eat at their homes to go around. Nancy was nineteen; Lou was twenty. Both were pretty, active, country girls who had no ambition to go on the stage.

The little cherub that sits up aloft guided them to a cheap and respectable boarding-house. Both found positions and became wage-earners. They remained chums. It is at the end of six months that I would beg you to step forward and be introduced to them. Meddlesome Reader: my Lady friends, Miss Nancy and Miss Lou. While you are shaking hands please take notice – cautiously – of their attire. Yes, cautiously; for they are as quick to resent a stare as a lady in a box at the horse show is.

Lou is a piecework ironer in a hand laundry. She is clothed in a badly-fitting purple dress, and her hat plume is four inches too long; but her ermine muff and scarf cost twenty-five dollars, and its fellow beasts will be ticketed in the windows at seven dollars ninety-eight cents before the season is over. Her cheeks are pink, and her light blue eyes bright. Contentment radiates from her.

Nancy you would call a shop-girl – because you have the habit. There is no type; but a perverse generation is always seeking a type; so this is what the type should be. She has the high-ratted pompadour, and the exaggerated straight-front. Her skirt is shoddy, but has the correct flare. No furs protect her against the bitter spring air, but she wears her short broadcloth jacket as jauntily as though it were Persian lamb! On her face and in her eyes, remorseless type-seeker, is the typical shop-girl expression. It is a look of silent but contemptuous revolt against cheated womanhood; of sad prophecy of the vengeance to come. When she laughs her loudest the look is still there. The same look can be seen in the eyes of Russian peasants; and those of us left will see it some day on Gabriel's face when he comes to blow us up. It is a look that should wither and abash man; but he has been known to smirk at it and offer flowers – with a string tied to them.

Now lift your hat and come away, while you receive Lou's cheery 'See you again,' and the sardonic, sweet smile of Nancy that seems, somehow, to miss you and go fluttering like a white moth up over the housetops to the stars.

The two waited on the corner for Dan. Dan was Lou's steady company. Faithful? Well, he was on hand when Mary would have had to hire a dozen subpoena servers to find her lamb.

'Ain't you cold, Nance?' said Lou. 'Say, what a chump you are for working in that old store for eight dollars a week! I made eighteen dollars fifty last week. Of course ironing ain't as swell work as selling lace behind a counter, but it pays. None of us ironers make less than ten dollars. And I don't know that it's any less respectful work, either.'

'You can have it,' said Nancy, with uplifted nose. 'I'll take my eight a week and hall-bedroom. I like to be among nice things and swell people. And look what a chance I've got! Why, one of our glove girls married a Pittsburg – steel maker, or blacksmith or something – the other day worth a million dollars. I'll catch a swell myself some time. I ain't bragging on my looks or anything; but I'll take my chances where there's big prizes offered. What show would a girl have in a laundry?'

'Why, that's where I met Dan,' said Lou triumphantly. 'He came in for his Sunday shirt and collars and saw me at the first board ironing. We all try to get to work at the first board. Ella Maginnis was sick that day, and I had her place. He said he noticed my arms first, how round and white they was. I had my sleeves rolled up. Some nice fellows come into laundries. You can tell 'em by their bringing their clothes in suitcases, and turning in the door sharp and sudden.'

'How can you wear a waist like that, Lou?' said Nancy, gazing down at the offending article with sweet scorn in her heavy-lidded eyes. 'It shows fierce taste.'

'This waist?' cried Lou, with wide-eyed indignation. 'Why, I paid sixteen dollars for this waist. It's worth twenty-five. A woman left it to be laundered, and never called for it. The boss sold it to me. It's got yards and yards of hand embroidery on it. Better talk about that ugly, plain thing you've got on.'

'This ugly, plain thing,' said Nancy calmly, 'was copied from one that Mrs Van Alstyne Fisher was wearing. The girls say her bill in the store last year was twelve thousand dollars. I made mine myself. It cost me one dollar fifty. Ten feet away you couldn't tell it from hers.'

'Oh, well,' said Lou good-naturedly, 'if you want to starve and put on airs, go ahead. But I'll take my job and good wages; and after hours give me something as fancy and attractive to wear as I am able to buy.'

But just then Dan came – a serious young man with a ready-made necktie, who had escaped the city's brand of frivolity – an electrician earning thirty dollars per week who looked upon Lou with the sad eyes of Romeo, and thought her embroidered waist a web in which any fly should delight to be caught.

'My friend, Mr Owens – shake hands with Miss Danforth,' said Lou.

'I'm mighty glad to know you, Miss Danforth,' said Dan, with outstretched hand. 'I've heard Lou speak of you so often.'

'Thanks,' said Nancy, touching his fingers with the tips of her cool ones, 'I've heard her mention you – a few times.'

Lou giggled.

'Did you get that handshake from Mrs Van Alstyne Fisher, Nance?' she asked.

'If I did, you can feel safe in copying it,' said Nancy.

'Oh, I couldn't use it at all. It's too stylish for me. It's intended to set off diamond rings, that high shake is. Wait till I get a few and then I'll try it.'

'Learn it first,' said Nancy wisely, 'and you'll be more likely to get the rings.'

'Now, to settle this argument,' said Dan with his ready, cheerful smile, 'let me make a proposition. As I can't take both of you up to Tiffany's and do the right thing, what do you say to a little vaudeville? I've got the tickets. How about looking at stage diamonds since we can't shake hands with the real sparklers?'

The faithful squire took his place close to the kerb; Lou next, a little peacocky in her bright and pretty clothes; Nancy on the inside, slender, and soberly clothed as the sparrow, but with the true Van Alstyne Fisher walk – thus they set out for their evening's moderate diversion.

I do not suppose that many look upon a great department store as an educational institution. But the one in which Nancy worked was something like that to her. She was surrounded by beautiful things that breathed of taste and refinement. If you live in an atmosphere of luxury, luxury is yours whether your money pays for it, or another's.

The people she served were mostly women whose dress, manners, and position in the social world were quoted as criterions. From them Nancy began to take toll – the best from each according to her view.

From one she would copy and practise a gesture, from another an eloquent lifting of an eyebrow, from others, a manner of walking, of carrying a purse, of smiling, of greeting a friend, of addressing 'inferiors in station.' From her best beloved model, Mrs Van Alstyne Fisher, she made requisition for that excellent thing, a soft, low voice as clear as silver and as perfect in articulation as the notes of a thrush. Suffused in the aura of this high social refinement and good breeding, it was impossible for her to escape a deeper effect of it. As good habits are said to be better than good principles, so, perhaps, good manners are better than good habits. The teachings of your parents may not keep alive your New England conscience; but if you sit on a straight-back chair and repeat the words 'prisms and pilgrims' forty times the devil will flee from you. And when Nancy spoke in the Van Alstyne Fisher tones she felt the thrill of *noblesse oblige* to her very bones.

There was another source of learning in the great departmental school. Whenever you see three or four shop-girls gather in a bunch and jingle their wire bracelets as an accompaniment to apparently frivolous conversation, do not think that they are there for the purpose of criticising the way Ethel does her back hair. The meeting may lack the dignity of the deliberative bodies of man; but it has all the importance of the occasion on which Eve and her first daughter first put their heads together to make Adam understand his proper place in the household. It is a Woman's Conference for Common Defence and Exchange of Strategical Theories of Attack and Repulse upon and against the World, which is a Stage, and Man, its Audience who Persists in Throwing Bouquets Thereupon. Woman, the most helpless of the young of any animal – with the fawn's grace but without its fleetness; with the bird's beauty but without its power of flight; with the honeybee's burden of sweetness but without its – Oh, let's drop that simile – some of us may have been stung.

During this council of war they pass weapons one to another, and exchange stratagems that each has devised and formulated out of the tactics of life.

'I says to 'im,' says Sadie, 'ain't you the fresh thing! Who do you suppose I am, to be addressing such a remark to me? And what do you think he says back to me?'

The heads, brown, black, flaxen, red and yellow bob together; the answer is given; and the parry to the thrust is decided upon, to be used by each thereafter in passages-at-arms with the common enemy, man.

Thus Nancy learned the art of defence; and to women successful defence means victory.

The curriculum of a department store is a wide one. Perhaps no other college could have fitted her as well for her life's ambition – the drawing of a matrimonial prize.

Her station in the store was a favoured one. The music-room was near enough for her to hear and become familiar with the works of the best composers – at least to acquire the familiarity that passed for appreciation in the social world in which she was vaguely trying to set a tentative and aspiring foot. She absorbed the educating influence of artwares, of costly and dainty fabrics, of adornments that are almost culture to women.

The other girls soon became aware of Nancy's ambition. 'Here comes your millionaire, Nance,' they would call to her whenever any man who looked the role approached her counter. It got to be a habit of men, who were hanging about while their womenfolk were shopping, to stroll over to the handkerchief counter and dawdle over the cambric squares. Nancy's imitation high-bred air and genuine dainty beauty was what attracted. Many men thus came to display their graces before her. Some of them may have been millionaires; others were certainly not more than their sedulous apes. Nancy learned to discriminate. There was a window at the end of the handkerchief counter; and she could see the rows of vehicles waiting for the shoppers in the street below. She looked, and perceived that automobiles differ as well as do their owners.

Once a fascinating gentleman bought four dozen handkerchiefs, and wooed her across the counter with a King Cophetua air. When he had gone one of the girls said: 'What's wrong, Nance, that you didn't warm up to that fellow? He looks the swell article, all right, to me.'

'Him?' said Nancy, with her coolest, sweetest, most impersonal, Van Alstyne Fisher smile; 'not for mine. I saw him drive up outside. A twelve-horsepower machine and an Irish chauffeur! And you saw what kind of handkerchiefs he bought – silk! And he's got dactylis on him. Give me the real thing or nothing, if you please.'

Two of the most 'refined' women in the store – a forelady and a cashier – had a few 'swell gentlemen friends' with whom they now and then dined. Once they included Nancy in an invitation. The dinner took place in a spectacular café whose tables are engaged for New Year's Eve a year in advance. There were two 'gentlemen friends' – one without any hair on his head – high living ungrew it; and we can prove it – the other a young man whose worth and sophistication he impressed upon you in two convincing ways – he swore that all the wine was corked; and he wore diamond cuff buttons. This young man perceived irresistible excellences in Nancy. His taste ran to showgirls; and here was one that added the voice and manner of his high social world to the franker charms of her own caste. So, on the following day, he appeared in the store and made her a serious proposal of marriage over a box of hemstitched, grass-bleached Irish linens. Nancy declined. A brown pompadour ten feet away had been using her eyes and ears. When the rejected suitor had gone she heaped carboys of upbraidings and horror upon Nancy's head.

'What a terrible little fool you are! That fellow's a millionaire – he's a nephew of old Van Skittles himself. And he was talking on the level, too. Have you gone crazy, Nance?'

'Have I?' said Nancy. 'I didn't take him, did I? He isn't a millionaire so hard that you could notice it, anyhow. His family only allows him $20,000 a year to spend. The bald-headed fellow was guying him about it the other night at supper.'

The brown pompadour came nearer and narrowed her eyes.

'Say, what do you want?' she enquired, in a voice hoarse for lack of chewing-gum. 'Ain't that enough for you? Do you want to be a Mormon, and marry Rockefeller and Gladstone Dowie and the King of Spain and the whole bunch? Ain't $20,000 a year good enough for you?'

Nancy flushed a little under the level gaze of the black, shallow eyes.

'It wasn't altogether the money, Carrie,' she explained. 'His friend caught him in a rank lie the other night at dinner. It was about some girl he said he hadn't been to the theatre with. Well, I can't stand a liar. Put everything together – I don't like him; and that settles it. When I sell out it's not going to be on any bargain day. I've got to have something that sits up in a chair like a man, anyhow. Yes, I'm looking out for a catch; but it's got to be able to do something more than make a noise like a toy bank.'

'The physiopathic ward for yours!' said the brown pompadour, walking away.

The high ideas, if not ideals – Nancy continued to cultivate on eight dollars per week. She bivouacked on the trail of the great unknown 'catch', eating her dry bread and tightening her belt day by day. On her face was the faint, soldierly, sweet, grim smile of the preordained man hunter. The store was her forest; and many times she raised her rifle at game that seemed broad-antlered and big; but always some deep, unerring instinct – perhaps of the huntress, perhaps of the woman – made her hold her fire and take up the trail again.

Lou flourished in the laundry. Out of her eighteen dollars fifty cents per week she paid six dollars for her room and board. The rest went mainly for clothes. Her opportunities for bettering her taste and manners were few compared with Nancy's. In the steaming laundry there was nothing but work, work and her thoughts of the evening pleasures to come. Many costly and showy fabrics passed under her iron; and it may be that her growing fondness for dress was thus transmitted to her through the conducting metal.

When the day's work was over Dan awaited her outside, her faithful shadow in whatever light she stood.

Sometimes he cast an honest and troubled glance at Lou's clothes that increased in conspicuity rather than in style; but this was no disloyalty; he deprecated the attention they called to her in the streets.

And Lou was no less faithful to her chum. There was a law that Nancy should go with them on whatsoever outings they might take. Dan bore the extra burden heartily and in good cheer. It might be said that Lou furnished the colour, Nancy the tone, and Dan the weight of the distraction-seeking trio. The escort, in his neat but obviously ready-made suit, his ready-made tie and unfailing, genial, ready-made wit never startled or clashed. He was of that good kind that you are likely to forget while they are present, but remember distinctly after they are gone.

To Nancy's superior taste the flavour of these ready-made pleasures was sometimes a little bitter: but she was young! and youth is a gourmand, when it cannot be a gourmet.

'Dan is always wanting me to marry him right away,' Lou told her once. 'But why should I? I'm independent. I can do as I please with the money I earn; and he never would agree for me to keep on working afterward. And say, Nance, what do you want to stick to that old store for, and half dress yourself? I could get you a place in the laundry right now if you'd come. It seems to me that you could afford to be a little less stuck-up if you could make a good deal more money.'

'I don't think I'm stuck-up, Lou,' said Nancy, 'but I'd rather live on half rations and stay where I am. I suppose I've got the habit. It's the chance that I want. I don't expect to be always behind a counter. I'm learning something new every day. I'm right up against refined and rich people all the time – even if I do only wait on them; and I'm not missing any pointers that I see passing around.'

'Caught your millionaire yet?' asked Lou, with her teasing laugh.

'I haven't selected one yet,' answered Nancy. 'I've been looking them over.'

'Goodness! the idea of picking over 'em! Don't you ever let one get by you, Nance – even if he's a few dollars shy. But of course you're joking – millionaires don't think about working girls like us.'

'It might be better for them if they did,' said Nancy, with cool wisdom. 'Some of us could teach them how to take care of their money.'

'If one was to speak to me,' laughed Lou, 'I know I'd have a duck-fit.'

'That's because you don't know any. The only difference between swells and other people is you have to watch 'em closer. Don't you think that red silk lining is just a little bit too bright for that coat, Lou?'

Lou looked at the plain, dull olive jacket of her friend.

'Well, no I don't – but it may seem so beside that faded-looking thing you've got on.'

'This jacket,' said Nancy complacently, 'has exactly the cut and fit of one that Mrs Van Alstyne Fisher was wearing the other day. The material cost me three dollars ninety-eight cents. I suppose hers cost about a hundred dollars more.'

'Oh, well,' said Lou lightly, 'it don't strike me as million-aire bait. Shouldn't wonder if I catch one before you do, anyway.'

Truly it would have taken a philosopher to decide upon the values of the theories held by the two friends. Lou, lacking that certain pride and fastidiousness that keeps stores and desks filled with girls working for the barest living, thumped away gaily with her iron in the noisy and stifling laundry. Her wages supported her even beyond the point of comfort; so that her dress profited until sometimes she cast a sidelong glance of impatience at the neat but inelegant apparel of Dan – Dan the constant, the immutable, the undeviating.

As for Nancy, her case was one of tens of thousands. Silk and jewels and laces and ornaments and the perfume and music of the fine world of good breeding and taste – these were made for woman; they are her equitable portion. Let her keep near them if they are a part of life to her, and if she will. She is no traitor to herself, as Esau was; for she keeps her birthright, and the pottage she earns is often very scant.

In this atmosphere Nancy belonged, and she throve in it and ate her frugal meals and schemed over her cheap dresses with a determined and contented mind. She already knew woman; and she was studying man, the animal, both as to his habits and eligibility. Some day she would bring down the game that she wanted; but she promised herself it would be what seemed to her the biggest and the best, and nothing smaller.

Thus she kept her lamp trimmed and burning to receive the bridegroom when he should come.

But another lesson she learned, perhaps unconsciously. Her standard of values began to shift and change. Sometimes the dollar-mark grew blurred in her mind's eye, and shaped itself into letters that spelled such words as 'truth' and 'honour' and now and then just 'kindness'. Let us make a likeness of one who hunts the moose or elk in some mighty wood. He sees a little dell, mossy and embowered, where a rill trickles, babbling to him of rest and comfort. At these times the spear of Nimrod himself grows blunt.

So Nancy wondered sometimes if Persian lamb was always quoted at its market value by the hearts that it covered.

One Thursday evening Nancy left the store and turned across Sixth Avenue, westward to the laundry. She was expected to go with Lou and Dan to a musical comedy.

Dan was just coming out of the laundry when she arrived. There was a queer, strained look on his face.

'I thought I would drop around to see if they had heard from her,' he said.

'Heard from who?' asked Nancy. 'Isn't Lou there?'

'I thought you knew,' said Dan. 'She hasn't been there or at the house where she lived since Monday. She moved all her things there. She told one of the girls in the laundry she might be going to Europe.'

'Hasn't anybody seen her anywhere?' asked Nancy.

Dan looked at her with his jaws set grimly and a steely gleam in his steady gray eyes.

'They told me in the laundry,' he said harshly, 'that they saw her pass yesterday – in an automobile. With one of the millionaires, I suppose, that you and Lou were for ever busying your brains about.'

For the first time Nancy quailed before a man. She laid her hand, that trembled slightly, on Dan's sleeve.

'You've no right to say such a thing to me, Dan – as if I had anything to do with it!'

'I didn't mean it that way,' said Dan, softening. He fumbled in his vest pocket.

'I've got the tickets for the show tonight,' he said, with a gallant show of lightness. 'If you—'

Nancy admired pluck whenever she saw it.

'I'll go with you, Dan,' she said.

Three months went by before Nancy saw Lou again.

At the twilight one evening the shop-girl was hurrying home along the border of a little quiet park. She heard her name called, and wheeled about in time to catch Lou rushing into her arms.

After the first embrace they drew their heads back as serpents do, ready to attack or to charm, with a thousand questions trembling on their swift tongues. And then Nancy noticed that prosperity had descended upon Lou, manifesting itself in costly furs, flashing gems, and creations of the tailor's art.

'You little fool!' cried Lou, loudly and affectionately. 'I see you are still working in that store, and as shabby as ever. And how about that big catch you were going to make – nothing doing yet, I suppose?'

And then Lou looked, and saw that something better than prosperity had descended upon Nancy – something that shone brighter than gems in her eyes and redder than a rose in her cheeks, and that danced like electricity anxious to be loosed from the tip of her tongue.

'Yes, I'm still in the store,' said Nancy, 'but I'm going to leave it next week. I've made my catch – the biggest catch in the world. You won't mind now, Lou, will you? – I'm going to be married to Dan – to Dan! – he's my Dan now – why, Lou!'

Around the corner of the park strolled one of those new-crop, smooth-faced young policemen that are making the force more endurable – at least to the eye. He saw a woman with an expensive fur coat and diamond-ringed hands crouching down against the iron fence of the park, sobbing turbulently, while a slender, plainly dressed working girl leaned close, trying to console her. But the Gibsonian cop, being of the new order, passed on, pretending not to notice, for he was wise enough to know that these matters are beyond help, so far as the power he represents is concerned, though he rap the pavement with his nightstick till the sound goes up to the farthermost stars.

'Little Speck in Garnered Fruit'

The honeymoon was at its full. There was a flat with the reddest of new carpets, tasselled portieres and six steins with pewter lids arranged on a ledge above the wainscoting of the dining-room. The wonder of it was yet upon them. Neither of them had ever seen a yellow primrose by the river's brim; but if such a sight had met their eyes at that time it would have seemed like – well, whatever the poet expected the right kind of people to see in it besides a primrose.

The bride sat in the rocker with her feet resting upon the world. She was wrapped in rosy dreams and a kimono of the same hue. She wondered what the people in Greenland and Tasmania and Baluchistan were saying one to another about her marriage to Kid McGarry. Not that it made any difference. There was no welterweight from London to the Southern Cross that could stand up four hours – no, four rounds – with her bridegroom. And he had been hers for three weeks; and the crook of her little finger could sway him more than the fist of any 142-pounder in the world.

Love, when it is ours, is the other name for self-abnegation and sacrifice. When it belongs to people across the airshaft it means arrogance and self-conceit.

The bride crossed her Oxfords and looked thoughtfully at the distemper Cupids on the ceiling.

'Precious,' said she, with the air of Cleopatra asking Antony for Rome done up in tissue-paper and delivered at residence, 'I think I would like a peach.'

Kid McGarry arose and put on his coat and hat. He was serious, shaven, sentimental and spry.

'All right,' said he, as coolly as though he were only agreeing to sign articles to fight the champion of England. 'I'll step down and cop one out for you – see?'

'Don't be long,' said the bride. 'I'll be lonesome without my naughty boy. Get a nice ripe one.'

After a series of farewells that would have befitted an imminent voyage to foreign parts, the Kid went down to the street.

Here he not unreasonably hesitated, for the season was yet early spring, and there seemed small chance of wrestling anywhere from those chill streets and stores the coveted luscious guerdon of summer's golden prime.

At the Italian's fruit-stand on the corner he stopped and cast a contemptuous eye over the display of papered oranges, highly polished apples and wan, sun-hungry bananas.

'Gotta da peach?' asked the Kid in the tongue of Dante, the lover of lovers.

'Ah, no,' sighed the vender. 'Not for one mont com-a da peach. Too soon. Gotta da nice-a orange. Like-a da orange?'

Scornful, the Kid pursued his quest. He entered the all-night chop-house, café, and bowling-alley of his friend and admirer, Justus O'Callahan. The O'Callahan was about in his institution, looking for leaks.

'I want it straight,' said the Kid to him. 'The old woman has got a hunch that she wants a peach. Now, if you've got a peach, Cal, get it out quick. I want it and others like it if you've got 'em in plural quantities.'

'The house is yours,' said O'Callahan. 'But there's no peach in it. It's too soon. I don't suppose you could even find 'em at one of the Broadway joints. That's too bad. When a lady fixes her mouth for a certain kind of fruit nothing else won't do. It's too late now to find any of the first-class fruiterers open. But if you think the missis would like some nice oranges, I've just got a box of fine ones in that she might—'

'Much obliged, Cal. It's a peach proposition right from the ring of the gong. I'll try farther.'

The time was nearly midnight as the Kid walked down the West-Side avenue. Few stores were open, and such as were practically hooted at the idea of a peach.

But in her moated flat the bride confidently awaited her Persian fruit. A champion welterweight not find a peach? – not stride triumphantly over the seasons and the zodiac and the almanac to fetch an Amsden's June or a Georgia cling to his owny-own?

The Kid's eye caught sight of a window that was lighted and gorgeous with Nature's most entrancing colours. The light suddenly went out. The Kid sprinted and caught the fruiterer locking his door.

'Peaches?' said he, with extreme deliberation.

'Well, no, sir. Not for three or four weeks yet. I haven't any idea where you might find some. There may be a few in town from under the glass, but they'd be hard to locate. Maybe at one of the more expensive hotels – some place where there's plenty of money to waste. I've got some very fine oranges, though – from a shipload that came in today.'

The Kid lingered on the corner for a moment, and then set out briskly toward a pair of green lights that flanked the steps of a building down a dark side-street.

'Captain around anywhere?' he asked of the desk sergeant of the police-station.

At that moment the Captain came briskly forward from the rear. He was in plain clothes, and had a busy air.

'Hello, Kid,' he said to the pugilist. 'Thought you were bridal-touring?'

'Got back yesterday. I'm a solid citizen now. Think I'll take an interest in municipal doings. How would it suit you to get into Denver Dick's place tonight, Cap?'

'Past performances,' said the Captain, twisting his moustache. 'Denver was closed up two months ago.'

'Correct,' said the Kid. 'Rafferty chased him out of the Forty-Third. He's running in your precinct now, and his game's bigger than ever. I'm down on this gambling business. I can put you against his game.'

'In my precinct?' growled the Captain. 'Are you sure, Kid? I'll take it as a favour. Have you got the entrée. How is it to be done?'

'Hammers,' said the Kid. 'They haven't got any steel on the doors yet. You'll need ten men. No; they won't let me in the place. Denver has been trying to do me. He thought I tipped him off for the other raid. I didn't though. You want to hurry. I've got to get back home. The house is only three blocks from here.'

Before ten minutes had sped the Captain with a dozen men stole with their guide into the hallway of a dark and virtuous-looking building in which businesses were conducted by day.

'Third floor, rear,' said the Kid softly. 'I'll lead the way.'

Two axemen faced the door that he pointed out to them.

'It seems all quiet,' said the Captain doubtfully. 'Are you sure your tip is straight?'

'Cut away!' said the Kid. 'It's on me if it ain't.'

The axes crashed through the as yet unprotected door. A blaze of light from within poured through the smashed panels. The door fell, and the raiders sprang into the room with their guns handy.

The big room was furnished with the gaudy magnificence dear to Denver Dick's western ideas. Various well-patronised games were in progress. About fifty men who were in the room rushed upon the police in a grand break for personal liberty. The plain-clothes men had to do a little club-swinging. More than half the patrons escaped.

Denver Dick had graced his game with his own presence that night. He led the rush that was intended to sweep away the smaller body of raiders. But when he saw the Kid his manner became personal. Being in the heavyweight class, he cast himself joyfully upon his slighter enemy, and they rolled down a flight of stairs in each other's arms. On the landing they separated and arose, and then the Kid was able to use some of his professional tactics, which had been useless to him while in the clutch of a 200-pound sporting gentleman who was about to lose $20,000 worth of paraphernalia.

After vanquishing his adversary, the Kid hurried upstairs and through the gambling-room into a smaller apartment connecting by an arched doorway.

Here was a long table set with choicest chinaware and silver, and lavishly furnished with food of that expensive and spectacular sort of which the devotees of sport are supposed to be fond. Here again was to be perceived the liberal and florid taste of the gentleman with the urban cognomenal prefix.

A No. 10 patent leather shoe protruded a few of its inches outside the tablecloth along the floor. The Kid seized this, and plucked forth a black man in a white tie and the garb of a servitor.

'Get up!' commanded the Kid. 'Are you in charge of this free lunch?'

'Yes, sah, I was. Has they done pinched us ag'in, boss?'

'Looks that way. Listen to me. Are there any peaches in this layout? If there ain't I'll have to throw up the sponge.'

'There was three dozen, sah, when the game opened this evinin'; but I reckon the gentlemen done eat 'em all up. If you'd like to eat a fust-rate orange, sah, I kin find you some.'

'Get busy,' ordered the Kid sternly, 'and move whatever peach crop you've got quick, or there'll be trouble. If anybody oranges me again tonight, I'll knock his face off.'

The raid on Denver Dick's high-priced and prodigal luncheon revealed one lone, last peach that had escaped the epicurean jaws of the followers of chance. Into the Kid's pocket it went, and that indefatlgable forager departed immediately with his prize. With scarcely a glance at the scene on the sidewalk below, where the officers were loading their prisoners into the patrol wagons, he moved homeward with long, swift strides.

His heart was light as he went. So rode the knights back to Camelot after perils and high deeds done for their ladies fair. The Kid's lady had commanded him and he had obeyed. True, it was but a peach that she had craved; but it had been no small deed to glean a peach at midnight from that wintry city where yet the February snows lay like iron. She had asked for a peach; she was his bride; in his pocket the peach was warming in his hand that held it for fear that it might fall out and be lost.

On the way the Kid turned in at an all-night drugstore and said to the spectacled clerk: 'Say, sport, I wish you'd size up this rib of mine and see if it's broke. I was in a little scrap, and bumped down a flight or two of stairs.'

The druggist made an examination.

'It isn't broken,' was his diagnosis; 'but you have a bruise there that looks like you'd fallen off the Flatiron twice.'

'That's all right,' said the Kid. 'Let's have your clothes-brush, please.'

The bride waited in the rosy glow of the pink lampshade. The miracles were not all passed away. By breathing a desire for some slight thing – a flower, a pomegranate, a – oh, yes, a peach – she could send forth her man into the night, into the world which could not withstand him, and he would do her bidding.

And now he stood by her chair and laid the peach in her hand.

'Naughty boy!' she said fondly. 'Did I say a peach? I think I would much rather have had an orange.'

Blest be the bride.

The Pendulum

'Eighty-First Street – let 'em out, please,' yelled the shepherd in blue.

A flock of citizen sheep scrambled out and another flock scrambled aboard. Ding-ding! The cattle cars of the Manhattan Elevated rattled away, and John Perkins drifted down the stairway of the station with the released flock.

John walked slowly toward his flat. Slowly, because in the lexicon of his daily life there was no such word as 'perhaps'. There are no surprises awaiting a man who has been married two years and lives in a flat. As he walked John Perkins prophesied to himself with gloomy and downtrodden cynicism the foregone conclusions of the monotonous day.

Katy would meet him at the door with a kiss flavoured with cold cream and butterscotch. He would remove his coat, sit upon a macadamised lounge and read, in the evening paper, of Russians and Japs slaughtered by the deadly Linotype. For dinner there would be pot roast; a salad flavoured with a dressing warranted not to crack or injure the leather, stewed rhubarb and the bottle of strawberry marmalade blushing at the certificate of chemical purity on its label. After dinner Katy would show him the new patch in her crazy quilt that the iceman had cut for her off the end of his four-in-hand. At half-past seven they would spread newspapers over the furniture to catch the pieces of plastering that fell when the fat man in the flat overhead began to take his physical culture exercises. Exactly at eight Hickey & Mooney, of the vaudeville team (unbooked) in the flat across the hall would yield to the gentle influence of delirium tremens and begin to overturn chairs under the delusion that Hammerstein was pursuing them with a five-hundred-dollar-a-week contract. Then the gent at the window across the air-shaft would get out his flute; the nightly gas leak would steal forth to frolic in the highways; the dumb waiter would slip off its trolley; the janitor would drive Mrs Zanowitski's five children once more across the Yalu, the lady with the champagne shoes and the Skye terrier would trip downstairs and paste her Thursday name over her bell and letter box – and the evening routine of the Frogmore flats would be under way.

John Perkins knew these things would happen. And he knew that at a quarter-past eight he would summon his nerve and reach for his hat, and that his wife would deliver this speech in a querulous tone: 'Now, where are you going, I'd like to know, John Perkins?'

'Thought I'd drop up to McCloskey's,' he would answer, 'and play a game or two of pool with the fellows.'

Of late such had been John Perkins' habit. At ten or eleven he would return. Sometimes Katy would be asleep; sometimes waiting up; ready to melt in the crucible of her ire a little more gold plating from the wrought-steel chains of matrimony. For these things Cupid will have to answer when he stands at the bar of justice with his victims from the Frogmore flats.

Tonight John Perkins encountered a tremendous upheaval of the commonplace when he reached his door. No Katy was there with her affectionate, confectionate kiss. The three rooms seemed in portentous disorder. All about lay her things in confusion. Shoes in the middle of the floor, curling tongs, hair bows, kimonos, powder-box, jumbled together on dresser and chairs – this was not Katy's way. With a sinking heart John saw the comb with a curling cloud of her brown hair among its teeth. Some unusual hurry and perturbation must have possessed her, for she always carefully placed these combings in the little blue base on the mantel, to be some day formed into the coveted feminine 'rat'.

Hanging conspicuously to the gas jet by a string was a folded paper. John seized it. It was a note from his wife running thus:

DEAR JOHN – I just had a telegram saying mother is very sick. I am going to take the 4.30 train. Brother Sam is going to meet me at the depot there. There is cold mutton in the icebox. I hope it isn't her quinsy again. Pay the milkman fifty cents. She had it bad last spring. Don't forget to write to the company about the gas meter, and your good socks are in the top drawer. I will write tomorrow.

Hastily,

KATY

Never during their two years of matrimony had he and Katy been separated for a night. John read the note over and over in a dumbfounded way. Here was a break in a routine that had never varied, and it left him dazed.

There on the back of a chair hung, pathetically empty and formless, the red wrapper with black dots that she always wore while getting the meals. Her weekday clothes had been tossed here and there in her haste. A little paper bag of her favourite butterscotch lay with its string yet unwound. A daily paper sprawled on the floor, gaping rectangularly where a railroad timetable had been clipped from it. Everything in the room spoke of a loss, of an essence gone, of its soul and life departed. John Perkins stood among the dead remains with a queer feeling of desolation in his heart.

He began to set the rooms tidy as well as he could. When he touched her clothes a thrill of something like terror went through him. He had never thought what existence would be without Katy. She had become so thoroughly annealed into his life that she was like the air he breathed – necessary but scarcely noticed. Now, without warning, she was gone, vanished, as completely absent as if she had never existed. Of course it would be only for a few days, or at most a week or two, but it seemed to him as if the very hand of death had pointed a finger at his secure and uneventful home.

John dragged the cold mutton from the icebox, made coffee and sat down to a lonely meal face to face with the strawberry marmalade's shameless certificate of purity. Bright among withdrawn blessings now appeared to him the ghosts of pot roast and the salad with tan polish dressing. His home was dismantled. A quinsied mother-in-law had knocked his lares and penates sky-high. After his solitary meal John sat at a front window.

He did not care to smoke. Outside the city roared to him to come join in its dance of folly and pleasure. The night was his. He might go forth unquestioned and thrum the strings of jollity as free as any gay bachelor there. He might carouse and wander and have his fling until dawn if he liked; and there would be no wrathful Katy waiting for him, bearing the chalice that held the dregs of his joy. He might play pool at McCloskey's with his roistering friends until Aurora dimmed the electric bulbs if he chose. The hymeneal strings that had curbed him always when the Frogmore flats had palled upon him were loosened. Katy was gone.

John Perkins was not accustomed to analysing his emotions. But as he sat in his Katy-bereft 10 x 12 parlour he hit unerringly upon the keynote of his discomfort. He knew now that Katy was necessary to his happiness. His feeling for her, lulled into unconsciousness by the dull round of domesticity, had been sharply stirred by the loss of her presence. Has it not been dinned into us by proverb and sermon and fable that we never prize the music till the sweet-voiced bird has flown – or in other no less florid and true utterances?

'I'm a double-dyed dub,' mused John Perkins, 'the way I've been treating Katy. Off every night playing pool and bumming with the boys instead of staying home with her. The poor girl here all alone with nothing to amuse her, and me acting that way! John Perkins, you're the worst kind of a shine. I'm going to make it up for the little girl. I'll take her out and let her see some amusement. And I'll cut out the McCloskey gang right from this minute.'

Yes, there was the city roaring outside for John Perkins to come dance in the train of Momus. And at McCloskey's the boys were knocking the balls idly into the pockets against the hour for the nightly game. But no primrose way nor clicking cue could woo the remorseful soul of Perkins, the bereft. The thing that was his, lightly held and half scorned, had been taken away from him, and he wanted it. Backward to a certain man named Adam, whom the cherubim bounced from the orchard, could Perkins, the remorseful, trace his descent.

Near the right hand of John Perkins stood a chair. On the back of it stood Katy's blue shirtwaist. It still retained something of her contour. Midway of the sleeves were fine, individual wrinkles made by the movements of her arms in working for his comfort and pleasure. A delicate but impelling odour of bluebells came from it. John took it and looked long and soberly at the unresponsive grenadine. Katy had never been unresponsive. Tears – yes, tears – came into John

Perkins' eyes. When she came back things would be different. He would make up for all his neglect. What was life without her?

The door opened. Katy walked in carrying a little hand satchel. John stared at her stupidly.

'My! I'm glad to get back,' said Katy. 'Ma wasn't sick to amount to anything. Sam was at the depot, and said she just had a little spell, and got all right soon after they telegraphed. So I took the next train back. I'm just dying for a cup of coffee.'

Nobody heard the click and the rattle of the cogwheels as the third-floor front of the Frogmore flats buzzed its machinery back into the Order of Things. A band slipped, a spring was touched, the gear was adjusted and the wheels revolved in their old orbits.

John Perkins looked at the clock. It was 8.15. He reached for his hat and walked to the door.

'Now, where are you going, I'd like to know, John Perkins?' asked Katy, in a querulous tone.

'Thought I'd drop up to McCloskey's,' said John, 'and play a game or two of pool with the fellows.'

Dougherty's Eye-Opener

Big Jim Dougherty was a sport. He belonged to that race of men. In Manhattan it is a distinct race. They are the Caribs of the North – strong, artful, self-sufficient, clannish, honourable within the laws of their race, holding in lenient contempt neighbouring tribes who bow to the measure of Society's tape-line. I refer, of course, to the titled nobility of sportdom. There is a class which bears as a qualifying adjective the substantive belonging to a wind instrument made of a cheap and base metal. But the tin mines of Cornwall never produced the material for manufacturing descriptive nomenclature for 'Big Jim' Dougherty.

The habitat of the sport is the lobby or the outside corner of certain hotels and combination restaurants and cafés. They are mostly men of different sizes, running from small to large; but they are unanimous in the possession of a recently shaven, blue-black cheek and chin and dark overcoats (in season) with black velvet collars.

Of the domestic life of the sport little is known. It has been said that Cupid and Hymen sometimes take a hand in the game and copper the queen of hearts to lose. Daring theorists have averred – not content with simply saying – that a sport often contracts a spouse, and even incurs descendants. Sometimes he sits in the game of politics; and then at chowder picnics there is a revelation of a Mrs Sport and little Sports in glazed hats with tin pails.

But mostly the sport is Oriental. He believes his womenfolk

should not be too patent. Somewhere behind grilles or flower-ornamented fire escapes they await him. There, no doubt, they tread on rugs from Teheran and are diverted by the bulbul and play upon the dulcimer and feed upon sweetmeats. But away from his home the sport is an integer. He does not, as men of other races in Manhattan do, become the convoy in his unoccupied hours of fluttering laces and high heels that tick off delectably the happy seconds of the evening parade. He herds with his own race at corners, and delivers a commentary in his Carib lingo upon the passing show.

'Big Jim' Dougherty had a wife, but he did not wear a button portrait of her upon his lapel. He had a home in one of those brownstone, iron-railed streets on the west side that look like a recently excavated bowling alley of Pompeii.

To this home of his Mr Dougherty repaired each night when the hour was so late as to promise no further diversion in the arch domains of sport. By that time the occupant of the monogamistic harem would be in dreamland, the bulbul silenced, and the hour propitious for slumber.

'Big Jim' always arose at twelve, meridian, for breakfast, and soon afterward he would return to the rendezvous of his 'crowd'.

He was always vaguely conscious that there was a Mrs Dougherty. He would have received without denial the charge that the quiet, neat, comfortable little woman across the table at home was his wife. In fact, he remembered pretty well that they had been married for nearly four years. She would often tell him about the cute tricks of Spot, the canary, and the light-haired lady that lived in the window of the flat across the street.

'Big Jim' Dougherty even listened to this conversation of hers sometimes. He knew that she would have a nice dinner ready for him every evening at seven when he came for it. She sometimes went to matinees, and she had a talking machine with six dozen records. Once when her Uncle Amos blew in on a wind from upstate, she went with him to the Eden Musée. Surely these things were diversions enough for any woman.

One afternoon, Mr Dougherty finished his breakfast, put on his hat, and got away fairly for the door. When his hand was on the knob he heard his wife's voice.

'Jim,' she said firmly, 'I wish you would take me out to dinner this evening. It has been three years since you have been outside the door with me.'

'Big Jim' was astounded. She had never asked anything like this before. It had the flavour of a totally new proposition. But he was a game sport.

'All right,' he said. 'You be ready when I come at seven. None of this "wait two minutes till I primp an hour or two" kind of business, now, Dele.'

'I'll be ready,' said his wife calmly.

At seven she descended the stone steps in the Pompeian bowling alley at the side of 'Big Jim' Dougherty. She wore a dinner gown made of a stuff that the spiders must have woven, and of a colour that a twilight sky must have contributed. A light coat with many admirably unnecessary capes and adorably inutile ribbons floated downward from her shoulders. Fine feathers do make fine birds; and the only reproach in the saying is for the man who refuses to give up his earnings to the ostrich-tip industry.

'Big Jim' Dougherty was troubled. There was a being at his side whom he did not know. He thought of the sober-hued plumage that this bird of paradise was accustomed to wear in her cage, and this winged revelation puzzled him. In some way she reminded him of the Delia Cullen that he had married four years before. Shyly and rather awkwardly he stalked at her right hand.

'After dinner I'll take you back home, Dele,' said Mr Dougherty, 'and then I'll drop back up to Seltzer's with the boys. You can have swell chuck tonight if you want it. I made a winning on Anaconda yesterday; so you can go as far as you like.'

Mr Dougherty had intended to make the outing with his unwonted wife an inconspicuous one. Uxoriousness was a weakness that the precepts of the Caribs did not countenance. If any of his friends of the track, the billiard cloth or the square circle had wives they had never complained of the fact in public. There were a number of *table d'hôte* places on the cross streets near the broad and shining way; and to one of these he had purposed to escort her so that the bushel might not be removed from the light of his domesticity.

But while on the way Mr Dougherty altered those intentions. He had been casting stealthy glances at his attractive companion, and he was seized with the conviction that she was no selling-plater. He resolved to parade with his wife past Seltzer's café, where at this time a number of his tribe would be gathered to view the daily evening procession. Yes; and he would take her to dine at Hoogley's, the swellest slow-lunch warehouse on the line, he said to himself.

The congregation of smooth-faced tribal gentlemen were on watch at Seltzer's. As Mr Dougherty and his reorganised Delia passed they stared, momentarily petrified, and then removed their hats – a performance as unusual to them as was the astonishing innovation presented to their gaze by 'Big Jim'. On the latter gentleman's impassive face there appeared a slight flicker of triumph – a faint flicker, no more to be observed than the expression called there by the draft of little casino to a four-card spade flush.

Hoogley's was animated. Electric lights shone – as, indeed, they were expected to do. And the napery, the glassware and the flowers also meritoriously performed the spectacular duties required of them. The guests were numerous, well-dressed and gay.

A waiter – not necessarily obsequious – conducted 'Big Jim' Dougherty and his wife to a table.

'Play that menu straight across for what you like, Dele,' said 'Big Jim'. 'It's you for a trough of the gilded oats tonight. It strikes me that maybe we've been sticking too fast to home fodder.'

'Big Jim's' wife gave her order. He looked at her with respect. She had mentioned truffles; and he had not known that she knew what truffles were. From the wine list she designated an appropriate and desirable brand. He looked at her with some admiration.

She was beaming with the innocent excitement that woman derives from the exercise of her gregariousness. She was talking to him about a hundred things with animation and delight. And as the meal progressed her cheeks, colourless from a life indoors, took on a delicate flush. 'Big Jim' looked around the room and saw that none of the women there had her charm. And then he thought of the three years she had suffered immurement, uncomplaining, and a flush of shame warmed him, for he carried fair play as an item in his creed.

But when the Honourable Patrick Corrigan, leader in Dougherty's district and a friend of his, saw them and came over to the table, matters got to the three-quarter stretch. The Honourable Patrick was a gallant man, both in deeds and words. As for the Blarney Stone, his previous actions toward it must have been pronounced. Heavy damages for breach of promise could surely have been obtained had the Blarney Stone seen fit to sue the Honourable Patrick.

'Jimmy, old man!' he called; he clapped Dougherty on the back; he shone like a midday sun upon Delia.

'Honourable Mr Corrigan – Mrs Dougherty,' said 'Big Jim'. The Honourable Patrick became a fountain of entertainment and admiration. The waiter had to fetch a third chair for him; he made another at the table, and the wine-glasses were refilled.

'You selfish old rascal!' he exclaimed, shaking an arch finger at 'Big Jim', 'to have kept Mrs Dougherty a secret from us.'

And then 'Big Jim' Dougherty, who was no talker, sat dumb, and saw the wife who had dined every evening for three years at home, blossom like a fairy flower. Quick, witty, charming, full of light and ready talk, she received the experienced attack of the Honourable Patrick on the field of repartee and surprised, vanquished, delighted him. She unfolded her long-closed petals, and around her the room became a garden. They tried to include 'Big Jim' in the conversation, but he was without a vocabulary.

And then a stray bunch of politicians and good fellows who lived for sport came into the room. They saw 'Big Jim' and the leader, and over they came and were made acquainted with Mrs Dougherty. And in a few minutes she was holding a salon. Half a dozen men surrounded her, courtiers all, and six found her capable of charming. 'Big Jim' sat, grim, and kept saying to himself: 'Three years, three years!'

The dinner came to an end. The Honourable Patrick reached for Mrs Dougherty's cloak; but that was a matter of action instead of words, and Dougherty's big hand got it first by two seconds.

While the farewells were being said at the door the Honourable Patrick smote Dougherty mightily between the shoulders.

'Jimmy, me boy,' he declared, in a giant whisper, 'the madam is a jewel of the first water. Ye're a lucky dog.'

'Big Jim' walked homeward with his wife. She seemed quite as pleased with the lights and show windows in the streets as with the admiration of the men in Hoogley's. As they passed Seltzer's they heard the sound of many voices in the café. The boys would be starting the drinks around now and discussing past performances.

At the door of their home Delia paused. The pleasure of the outing radiated softly from her countenance. She could not hope for Jim of evenings, but the glory of this one would lighten her lonely hours for a long time.

'Thank you for taking me out, Jim,' she said gratefully. 'You'll be going back up to Seltzer's now, of course.'

'To — with Seltzer's,' said 'Big Jim' emphatically. 'And d— Pat Corrigan! Does he think I haven't got any eyes?'

And the door closed behind both of them.

A Harlem Tragedy

Harlem.

Mrs Fink has dropped into Mrs Cassidy's flat one flight below.

'Ain't it a beaut?' said Mrs Cassidy.

She turned her face proudly for her friend Mrs Fink to see. One eye was nearly closed, with a great, greenish-purple bruise around it. Her lip was cut and bleeding a little and there were red fingermarks on each side of her neck.

'My husband wouldn't ever think of doing that to me,' said Mrs Fink, concealing her envy.

'I wouldn't have a man,' declared Mrs Cassidy, 'that didn't beat me up at least once a week. Shows he thinks something of you. Say! but that last dose Jack gave me wasn't no homoeopathic one. I can see stars yet. But he'll be the sweetest man in town for the rest of the week to make up for it. This eye is good for theatre tickets and a silk shirtwaist at the very least.'

'I should hope,' said Mrs Fink, assuming complacency, 'that Mr Fink is too much of a gentleman ever to raise his hand against me.'

'Oh, go on, Maggie!' said Mrs Cassidy, laughing and applying witch hazel, 'you're only jealous. Your old man is too frapped and slow to ever give you a punch. He just sits down and practises physical culture with a newspaper when he comes home – now ain't that the truth?'

'Mr Fink certainly peruses of the papers when he comes

home,' acknowledged Mrs Fink, with a toss of her head; 'but he certainly don't ever make no Steve O'Donnell out of me just to amuse himself – that's a sure thing.'

Mrs Cassidy laughed the contented laugh of the guarded and happy matron. With the air of Cornelia exhibiting her jewels, she drew down the collar of her kimono and revealed another treasured bruise, maroon-coloured, edged with olive and orange – a bruise now nearly well, but still to memory dear.

Mrs Fink capitulated. The formal light in her eye softened to envious admiration. She and Mrs Cassidy had been chums in the downtown paper-box factory before they had married, one year before. Now she and her man occupied the flat above Mame and her man. Therefore she could not put on airs with Mame.

'Don't it hurt when he soaks you?' asked Mrs Fink curiously.

'Hurt!' – Mrs Cassidy gave a soprano scream of delight. 'Well, say did you ever have a brick house fall on you? – well, that's just the way it feels – just like when they're digging you out of the ruins. Jack's got a left that spells two matinees and a new pair of Oxfords – and his right! – well, it takes a trip to Coney and six pairs of openwork, silk lisle threads to make that good.'

'But what does he beat you for?' enquired Mrs Fink, with wide-open eyes.

'Silly!' said Mrs Cassidy, indulgently. 'Why, because he's full. It's generally on Saturday nights.'

'But what cause do you give him?' persisted the seeker after knowledge.

'Why, didn't I marry him? Jack comes in tanked up; and I'm here, ain't I? Who else has he got a right to beat? I'd just like to catch him once beating anybody else! Sometimes it's because supper ain't ready; and sometimes it's because it is. Jack ain't particular about causes. He just lushes till he remembers he's married, and then he makes for home and does me up. Saturday nights I just move the furniture with sharp corners out of the way, so I won't cut my head when he gets his work in. He's got a left swing that jars you! Sometimes I take the count in the first round; but when I feel like having a good time during the week, or want some new rags, I come up again for more punishment. That's what I done last night. Jack knows I've been wanting a black silk waist for a month, and I didn't think just one black eye would bring it. Tell you what, Mag, I'll bet you the ice cream he brings it tonight.'

Mrs Fink was thinking deeply.

'My Mart,' she said, 'never hit me a lick in his life. It's just like you said, Mame; he comes in grouchy and ain't got a word to say. He never takes me out anywhere. He's a chair-warmer at home for fair. He buys me things, but he looks so glum about it that I never appreciate 'em.'

Mrs Cassidy slipped an arm around her chum.

'You poor thing!' she said. 'But everybody can't have a husband like Jack. Marriage wouldn't be no failure if they was all like him. These discontented wives you hear about – what they need is a man to come home and kick their slats in once a week, and then make it up in kisses and chocolate creams. That'd give 'em some interest in life. What I want is a masterful man that slugs you when he's jagged and hugs you when he ain't jagged. Preserve me from the man that ain't got the sand to do neither!'

Mrs Fink sighed.

The hallways were suddenly filled with sound. The door flew open at the kick of Mr Cassidy. His arms were occupied with bundles. Mame flew and hung about his neck. Her sound eye sparkled with the love-light that shines in the eye of the Maori maid when she recovers consciousness in the hut of the wooer who has stunned and dragged her there.

'Hello, old girl!' shouted Mr Cassidy. He shed his bundles and lifted her off her feet in a mighty hug. 'I got tickets for Barnum & Bailey's, and if you'll bust the string of one of them bundles I guess you'll find that silk waist – why, good-evening, Mrs Fink, I didn't see you at first. How's old Mart coming along?'

'He's very well, Mr Cassidy – thanks,' said Mrs Fink. 'I must be going along up now. Mart'll be home for supper soon. I'll bring you down that pattern you wanted tomorrow, Mame.'

Mrs Fink went up to her flat and had a little cry. It was a meaningless cry, the kind of cry that only a woman knows about, a cry from no particular cause, altogether an absurd cry; the most transient and the most hopeless cry in the repertory of grief. Why had Martin never thrashed her? He was as big and strong as Jack Cassidy. Did he not care for her at all? He never quarrelled; he came home and lounged about, silent, glum, idle. He was a fairly good provider, but he ignored the spices of life.

Mrs Fink's ship of dreams was becalmed. Her captain ranged between plum-duff and his hammock. If only he would shiver his timbers or stamp his foot on the quarterdeck now and then! And she had thought to sail so merrily, touching at ports in the Delectable Isles! But now, to vary the figure, she was ready to throw up the sponge, tired out, with a scratch to show for all those tame rounds with her sparring partner. For one moment she almost hated Mame – Mame, with her cuts and bruises, her salve of presents and kisses, her stormy voyage with her fighting, brutal, loving mate.

Mr Fink came home at seven. He was permeated with the curse of domesticity. Beyond the portal of his cosy home he cared not to roam. He was the man who had caught the street-car, the anaconda that had swallowed its prey, the tree that lay as it had fallen.

'Like the supper, Mart?' asked Mrs Fink, who had striven over it.

'M–m–m–yep,' grunted Mr Fink.

After supper he gathered his newspapers to read. He sat in his stockinged feet.

Arise, some new Dante, and sing me the befitting corner of perdition for the man who sitteth in the house in his stockinged feet! Sisters of Patience who by reason of ties or duty have endured it in silk, yarn, cotton, lisle thread or woollen – does not the new canto belong?

The next day was Labour Day. The occupations of Mr Cassidy and Mr Fink ceased for one passage of the sun. Labour, triumphant, would parade and otherwise disport itself.

Mrs Fink took Mrs Cassidy's pattern down early. Mame had on her new silk waist. Even her damaged eye managed to emit a holiday gleam. Jack was fruitfully penitent, and there was an hilarious scheme for the day afoot, with parks and picnics and Pilsener in it.

A rising, indignant jealousy seized Mrs Fink as she returned to her flat above. Oh, happy Mame, with her bruises and her quick-following balm! But was Mame to have a monopoly of happiness? Surely Martin Fink was as good a man as Jack Cassidy. Was his wife to go always unbelaboured and uncaressed? A sudden, brilliant, breathless idea came to Mrs Fink. She would show Mame that there were husbands as able to use their fists and perhaps to be as tender afterward as any Jack.

The holiday promised to be a nominal one with the Finks. Mrs Fink had the stationary washtubs in the kitchen filled with a two weeks' wash that had been soaking overnight. Mr Fink sat in his stockinged feet reading a newspaper. Thus Labour Day presaged to speed.

Jealousy surged high in Mrs Fink's heart, and higher still surged an audacious resolve. If her man would not strike her – if he would not so far prove his manhood, his prerogative and his interest in conjugal affairs, he must be prompted to his duty.

Mr Fink lit his pipe and peacefully rubbed an ankle with a stockinged toe. He reposed in the state of matrimony like a limp of unblended suet in a pudding. This was his level Elysium – to sit at ease vicariously girdling the world in print amid the wifely splashing of suds and the agreeable smells of breakfast dishes departed and dinner ones to come. Many ideas were far from his mind; but the furthest one was the thought of beating his wife.

Mrs Fink turned on the hot water and set the washboards in the suds. Up from the flat below came the gay laugh of Mrs Cassidy. It sounded like a taunt, a flaunting of her own happiness in the face of the unslugged bride above. Now was Mrs Fink's time.

Suddenly she turned like a fury upon the man reading.

'You lazy loafer!' she cried, 'must I work my arms off washing and toiling for the ugly likes of you? Are you a man or are you a kitchen hound?'

Mr Fink dropped his paper, motionless from surprise. She feared that he would not strike – that the provocation had been insufficient. She leaped at him and struck him fiercely in the face with her clenched hand. In that instant she felt a thrill of love for him such as she had not felt for many a day.

Rise up, Martin Fink, and come into your kingdom! Oh, she must feel the weight of his hand now – just to show that he cared – just to show that he cared!

Mr Fink sprang to his feet – Maggie caught him again on the jaw with a wide swing of her other hand. She closed her eyes in that fearful, blissful moment before his blow should come – she whispered his name to herself – she leaned to the expected shock, hungry for it.

In the flat below, Mr Cassidy, with a shamed and contrite face, was powdering Mame's eye in preparation for their junket. From the flat above came the sound of a woman's voice, high-raised, a bumping, a stumbling and a shuffling, a chair overturned – unmistakable sounds of domestic conflict.

'Mart and Mag scrapping?' postulated Mr Cassidy. 'Didn't know they ever indulged. Shall I trot up and see if they need a sponge-holder?'

One of Mrs Cassidy's eyes sparkled like a diamond. The other twinkled at least like paste.

'Oh, oh,' she said softly and without apparent meaning, in the feminine ejaculatory manner. 'I wonder if – I wonder if! Wait, Jack, till I go up and see.'

Up the stairs she sped. As her foot struck the hallway above, out from the kitchen door of her flat wildly flounced Mrs Fink.

'Oh, Maggie,' cried Mrs Cassidy, in a delighted whisper; 'did he? Oh, did he?'

Mrs Fink ran and laid her face upon her chum's shoulder and sobbed hopelessly.

Mrs Cassidy took Maggie's face between her hands and lifted it gently. Tear-stained it was, flushing and paling, but its velvety, pink-and-white, becomingly freckled surface was unscratched, unbruised, unmarred by the recreant fist of Mr Fink.

'Tell me, Maggie,' pleaded Mame, 'or I'll go in there and find out. What was it? Did he hurt you – what did he do?'

Mrs Fink's face went down again despairingly on the bosom of her friend.

'For Gawd's sake don't open that door, Mame,' she sobbed. 'And don't ever tell nobody – keep it under your hat. He – he never touched me, and – he's – oh, Gawd – he's washin' the clothes – he's washin' the clothes!'

Brickdust Row

Blinker was displeased. A man of less culture and poise and wealth would have sworn. But Blinker always remembered that he was a gentleman – a thing that no gentleman should do. So he merely looked bored and sardonic while he rode in a hansom to the centre of disturbance, which was the Broadway office of Lawyer Oldport, who was agent for the Blinker estate.

'I don't see,' said Blinker, 'why I should be always signing confounded papers. I am packed, and was to have left for the North Woods this morning. Now I must wait until tomorrow morning. I hate night trains. My best razors are, of course, at the bottom of some unidentifiable trunk. It is a plot to drive me to bay rum and a monologueing, thumb-handed barber. Give me a pen that doesn't scratch. I hate pens that scratch.'

'Sit down,' said double-chinned, gray Lawyer Oldport. 'The worst has not been told you. Oh, the hardships of the rich! The papers are not yet ready to sign. They will be laid before you tomorrow at eleven. You will miss another day. Twice shall the barber tweak the helpless nose of a Blinker. Be thankful that your sorrows do not embrace a haircut.'

'If,' said Blinker, rising, 'the act did not involve more signing of papers I would take my business out of your hands at once. Give me a cigar, please.'

'If,' said Lawyer Oldport, 'I had cared to see an old friend's son gulped down at one mouthful by sharks I would have ordered you to take it away long ago. Now, let's quit fooling,

Alexander. Besides the grinding task of signing your name some thirty times tomorrow, I must impose upon you the consideration of a matter of business – of business, and I may say humanity or right. I spoke to you about this five years ago, but you would not listen – you were in a hurry for a coaching trip, I think. The subject has come up again. The property—'

'Oh, property!' interrupted Blinker. 'Dear Mr Oldport, I think you mentioned tomorrow. Let's have it all at one dose tomorrow – signatures and property and snappy rubber bands and that smelly sealing-wax and all. Have luncheon with me? Well, I'll try to remember to drop in at eleven tomorrow. Morning.'

The Blinker wealth was in lands, tenements and hereditaments, as the legal phrase goes. Lawyer Oldport had once taken Alexander in his little pulmonary gasoline runabout to see the many buildings and rows of buildings that he owned in the city. For Alexander was sole heir. They had amused Blinker very much. The houses looked so incapable of producing the big sums of money that Lawyer Oldport kept piling up in banks for him to spend.

In the evening Blinker went to one of his clubs, intending to dine. Nobody was there except some old fogies playing whist who spoke to him with grave politeness and glared at him with savage contempt. Everybody was out of town. But here he was kept in like a schoolboy to write his name over and over on pieces of paper. His wounds were deep.

Blinker turned his back on the fogies, and said to the club steward who had come forward with some nonsense about cold fresh salmon roe: 'Symons, I'm going to Coney Island.' He said it as one might say: 'All's off; I'm going to jump into the river.'

The joke pleased Symons. He laughed within a sixteenth

of a note of the audibility permitted by the laws governing employees.

'Certainly, sir,' he tittered. 'Of course, sir, I think I can see you at Coney, Mr Blinker.'

Blinker got a paper and looked up the movements of Sunday steamboats. Then he found a cab at the first corner and drove to a North River pier. He stood in line, as democratic as you or I, and bought a ticket, and was trampled upon and shoved forward until, at last, he found himself on the upper deck of the boat staring brazenly at a girl who sat alone upon a camp stool. But Blinker did not intend to be brazen; the girl was so wonderfully good-looking that he forgot for one minute that he was the prince incog, and behaved just as he did in society.

She was looking at him, too, and not severely. A puff of wind threatened Blinker's straw hat. He caught it warily and settled it again. The movement gave the effect of a bow. The girl nodded and smiled, and in another instant he was seated at her side. She was dressed all in white, she was paler than Blinker imagined milkmaids and girls of humble stations to be, but she was as tidy as a cherry blossom, and her steady, supremely frank gray eyes looked out from the intrepid depths of an unshadowed and untroubled soul.

'How dare you raise your hat to me?' she asked, with a smile-redeemed severity.

'I didn't,' Blinker said, but he quickly covered the mistake by extending it to 'I didn't know how to keep from it after I saw you.'

'I do not allow gentlemen to sit by me to whom I have not been introduced,' she said, with a sudden haughtiness that deceived him. He rose reluctantly, but her clear, teasing laugh brought him down to his chair again.

'I guess you weren't going far,' she declared, with beauty's magnificent self-confidence.

'Are you going to Coney Island?' asked Blinker.

'Me?' She turned upon him wide-open eyes full of bantering surprise. 'Why, what a question! Can't you see that I'm riding a bicycle in the park?' Her drollery took the form of impertinence.

'And I am laying brick on a tall factory chimney,' said Blinker. 'Mayn't we see Coney together? I'm all alone and I've never been there before.'

'It depends,' said the girl, 'on how nicely you behave. I'll consider your application until we get there.'

Blinker took pains to provide against the rejection of his application. He strove to please. To adopt the metaphor of his nonsensical phrase, he laid brick upon brick on the tall chimney of his devoirs until, at length, the structure was stable and complete. The manners of the best society come around finally to simplicity; and as the girl's way was that naturally, they were on a mutual plane of communication from the beginning.

He learned that she was twenty, and her name was Florence; that she trimmed hats in a millinery shop; that she lived in a furnished room with her best chum, Ella, who was cashier in a shoe store; and that a glass of milk from the bottle on the windowsill and an egg that boils itself while you twist up your hair makes a breakfast good enough for anyone. Florence laughed when she heard 'Blinker'.

'Well,' she said. 'It certainly shows that you have imagination. It gives the "Smiths" a chance for a little rest, anyhow.'

They landed at Coney, and were dashed on the crest of a great human wave of mad pleasure-seekers into the walks and avenues of Fairyland gone into vaudeville.

With a curious eye, a critical mind and a fairly withheld judgement, Blinker considered the temples, pagodas and kiosks of popularised delights. Hoi polloi trampled, hustled and crowded him. Basket parties bumped him; sticky children tumbled, howling, under his feet, candying his clothes. Insolent youths strolling among the booths with hard-won canes under one arm and easily won girls on the other, blew defiant smoke from cheap cigars into his face. The publicity gentlemen with megaphones, each before his own stupendous attraction, roared like Niagara in his ears. Music of all kinds that could be tortured from brass, reed, hide or string, fought in the air to gain space for its vibrations against its competitors. But what held Blinker in awful fascination was the mob, the multitude, the proletariat, shrieking, struggling, hurrying, panting, hurling itself in incontinent frenzy, with unabashed abandon, into the ridiculous sham palaces of trumpery and tinsel pleasures. The vulgarity of it, its brutal overriding of all the tenets of repression and taste that were held by his caste, repelled him strongly.

In the midst of his disgust he turned and looked down at Florence by his side. She was ready with her quick smile and upturned, happy eyes, as bright and clear as the water in trout pools. The eyes were saying that they had the right to be shining and happy, for was their owner not with her (for the present) Man, her Gentleman Friend and holder of the keys to the enchanted city of fun?

Blinker did not read her look accurately, but by some miracle he suddenly saw Coney aright.

He no longer saw a mass of vulgarians seeking gross joys. He now looked clearly upon a hundred thousand true idealists. Their offences were wiped out. Counterfeit and false though the garish joys of these spangled temples were, he perceived that deep under the gilt surface they offered saving and apposite balm and satisfaction to the restless human heart. Here, at least, was the husk of Romance, the empty but shining casque of Chivalry, the breath-catching though safeguarded dip and flight of Adventure, the magic carpet that transports you to the realms of Fairyland, though its journey be through but a few poor yards of space. He no longer saw a rabble, but his brothers seeking the ideal. There was no magic of poesy here or of art; but the glamour of their imagination turned yellow calico into cloth of gold and the megaphones into the silver trumpets of joy's heralds.

Almost humbled, Blinker rolled up the shirtsleeves of his mind and joined the idealists.

'You are the lady doctor,' he said to Florence. 'How shall we go about doing this jolly conglomeration of fairy tales, incorporated?'

'We will begin there,' said the Princess, pointing to a fun pagoda on the edge of the sea, 'and we will take them all in, one by one.'

They caught the eight o'clock returning boat and sat, filled with pleasant fatigue against the rail in the bow, listening to the Italians' fiddle and harp. Blinker had thrown off all care. The North Woods seemed to him an uninhabitable wilderness. What a fuss he had made over signing his name – pooh! he could sign it a hundred times. And her name was as pretty as she was – 'Florence,' he said it to himself a great many times.

As the boat was nearing its pier in the North River a two-funnelled, drab, foreign-looking, seagoing steamer was dropping down toward the bay. The boat turned its nose in toward its slip. The steamer veered as if to seek midstream, and then yawed, seemed to increase its speed and struck the

Coney boat on the side near the stern, cutting into it with a terrifying shock and crash.

While the six hundred passengers on the boat were mostly tumbling about the decks in a shrieking panic the captain was shouting at the steamer that it should not back off and leave the rent exposed for the water to enter. But the steamer tore its way out like a savage sawfish and cleaved its heartless way, full speed ahead.

The boat began to sink at its stern, but moved slowly toward the slip. The passengers were a frantic mob, unpleasant to behold.

Blinker held Florence tightly until the boat had righted itself. She made no sound or sign of fear. He stood on a camp stool, ripped off the slats above his head and pulled down a number of the life preservers. He began to buckle one around Florence. The rotten canvas split and the fraudulent granulated cork came pouring out in a stream. Florence caught a handful of it and laughed gleefully.

'It looks like breakfast food,' she said. 'Take it off. They're no good.'

She unbuckled it and threw it on the deck. She made Blinker sit down, and sat by his side and put her hand in his. 'What'll you bet we don't reach the pier all right?' she said, and began to hum a song.

And now the captain moved among the passengers and compelled order. The boat would undoubtedly make her slip, he said, and ordered the women and children to the bow, where they could land first. The boat, very low in the water at the stern, tried gallantly to make his promise good.

'Florence,' said Blinker, as she held him close by an arm and hand, 'I love you.'

'That's what they all say,' she replied lightly.

'I am not one of "they all",' he persisted. 'I never knew anyone I could love before. I could pass my life with you and be happy every day. I am rich. I can make things all right for you.'

'That's what they all say,' said the girl again, weaving the words into her little, reckless song.

'Don't say that again,' said Blinker in a tone that made her look at him in frank surprise.

'Why shouldn't I say it?' she asked calmly. 'They all do.'

'Who are "they"?' he asked, jealous for the first time in his existence.

'Why, the fellows I know.'

'Do you know so many?'

'Oh, well, I'm not a wallflower,' she answered with modest complacency.

'Where do you see these – these men? At your home?'

'Of course not. I meet them just as I did you. Sometimes on the boat, sometimes in the park, sometimes on the street. I'm a pretty good judge of a man. I can tell in a minute if a fellow is one who is likely to get fresh.'

'What do you mean by "fresh"?'

'Why, try to kiss you – me, I mean.'

'Do any of them try that?" asked Blinker, clenching his teeth.

'Sure. All men do. You know that.'

'Do you allow them?'

'Some. Not many. They won't take you out anywhere unless you do.'

She turned her head and looked searchingly at Blinker. Her eyes were as innocent as a child's. There was a puzzled look in them, as though she did not understand him.

'What's wrong about my meeting fellows?' she asked, wonderingly.

'Everything,' he answered, almost savagely. 'Why don't you entertain your company in the house where you live? Is it necessary to pick up Tom, Dick and Harry on the streets?'

She kept her absolutely ingenuous eyes upon his.

'If you could see the place where I live you wouldn't ask that. I live in Brickdust Row. They call it that because there's red dust from the bricks crumbling over everything. I've lived there for more than four years. There's no place to receive company. You can't have anybody come to your room. What else is there to do? A girl has got to meet the men, hasn't she?'

'Yes,' he said hoarsely. 'A girl has got to meet a – has got to meet the men.'

'The first time one spoke to me on the street,' she continued, 'I ran home and cried all night. But you get used to it. I meet a good many nice fellows at church. I go on rainy days and stand in the vestibule until one comes up with an umbrella. I wish there was a parlour, so I could ask you to call, Mr Blinker – are you really sure it isn't "Smith", now?'

The boat landed safely. Blinker had a confused impression of walking with the girl through quiet cross-town streets until she stopped at a corner and held out her hand.

'I live just one more block over,' she said. 'Thank you for a very pleasant afternoon.'

Blinker muttered something and plunged northward till he found a cab. A big, gray church loomed slowly at his right. Blinker shook his fist at it through the window.

'I gave you a thousand dollars last week,' he cried under his breath, 'and she meets them in your very doors. There is something wrong; there is something wrong.'

At eleven the next day Blinker signed his name thirty times with a new pen provided by Lawyer Oldport.

'Now let me go to the woods,' he said surlily.

'You are not looking well,' said Lawyer Oldport. 'The trip will do you good. But listen, if you will, to that little matter of business of which I spoke to you yesterday, and also five years ago. There are some buildings, fifteen in number, of which there are new five-year leases to be signed. Your father contemplated a change in the lease provisions, but never made it. He intended that the parlours of these houses should not be sub-let, but that the tenants should be allowed to use them for reception rooms. These houses are in the shopping district, and are mainly tenanted by young working girls. As it is they are forced to seek companionship outside. This row of red brick—'

Blinker interrupted him with a loud, discordant laugh.

'Brickdust Row for an even hundred,' he cried. 'And I own it. Have I guessed right?'

'The tenants have some such name for it,' said Lawyer Oldport.

Blinker arose and jammed his hat down to his eyes.

'Do what you please with it,' he said harshly. 'Remodel it, burn it, raze it to the ground. But, man, it's too late, I tell you. It's too late. It's too late. It's too late.'

The Lost Blend

Since the bar has been blessed by the clergy, and cocktails open the dinners of the elect one may speak of the saloon. Teetotalers need not listen, if they choose; there is always the slot restaurant, where a dime dropped into the cold bouillon aperture will bring forth a dry Martini.

Con Lantry worked on the sober side of the bar in Kenealy's café. You and I stood, one-legged like geese, on the other side and went into voluntary liquidation with our week's wages. Opposite danced Con, clean, temperate, clear-headed, polite, white-jacketed, punctual, trustworthy, young, responsible, and took our money.

The saloon (whether blessed or cursed) stood in one of those little 'places' which are parallelograms instead of streets, and inhabited by laundries, decayed Knickerbocker families and Bohemians who have nothing to do with either

Over the café lived Kenealy and his family. His daughter Katherine had eyes of dark Irish – but why should you be told? Be content with your Geraldine or your Eliza Ann. For Con dreamed of her; and when she called softly at the foot of the back stairs for the pitcher of beer for dinner, his heart went up and down like a milk punch in the shaker. Orderly and fit are the rules of Romance; and if you hurl the last shilling of your fortune upon the bar for whisky, the bartender shall take it, and marry his boss's daughter, and good will grow out of it.

But not so Con. For in the presence of woman he was tongue-tied and scarlet. He who would quell with his eye the sonorous youth whom the claret punch made loquacious, or smash with lemon squeezer the obstreperous, or hurl gutter-wards the cantankerous without a wrinkle coming to his white lawn tie, when he stood before woman he was voiceless, incoherent, stuttering, buried beneath a hot avalanche of bashfulness and misery. What, then, was he before Katherine? A trembler, with no word to say for himself, a stone without blarney, the dumbest lover that ever babbled of the weather in the presence of his divinity.

There came to Kenealy's two sunburned men, Riley and McQuirk. They had conference with Kenealy; and then they took possession of a back room which they filled with bottles and siphons and jugs and druggist's measuring glasses. All the appurtenances and liquids of a saloon were there, but they dispensed no drinks. All day long the two sweltered in there, pouring and mixing unknown brews and decoctions from the liquors in their store. Riley had the education, and he figured on reams of paper, reducing gallons to ounces and quarts to fluid drams. McQuirk, a morose man with a red eye, dashed each unsuccessful completed mixture into the waste pipes with curses gentle, husky and deep. They laboured heavily and untiringly to achieve some mysterious solution, like two alchemists striving to resolve gold from the elements.

Into this back room one evening when his watch was done sauntered Con. His professional curiosity had been stirred by these occult bartenders at whose bar none drank, and who daily drew upon Kenealy's store of liquors to follow their consuming and fruitless experiments.

Down the back stairs came Katherine with her smile like sunrise on Gweebarra Bay.

'Good evening, Mr Lantry,' says she. 'And what is the news today, if you please?'

'It looks like r–rain,' stammered the shy one, backing to the wall.

'It couldn't do better,' said Katherine. 'I'm thinking there's nothing the worse off for a little water.'

In the back room Riley and McQuirk toiled like bearded witches over their strange compounds. From fifty bottles they drew liquids carefully measured after Riley's figures, and shook the whole together in a great glass vessel. Then McQuirk would dash it out, with gloomy profanity, and they would begin again.

'Sit down,' said Riley to Con, 'and I'll tell you.

'Last summer me and Tim concludes that an American bar in this nation of Nicaragua would pay. There was a town on the coast where there's nothing to eat but quinine and nothing to drink but rum. The natives and foreigners lay down with chills and get up with fevers; and a good mixed drink is nature's remedy for all such tropical inconveniences.

'So we lays in a fine stock of wet goods in New York, and bar fixtures and glassware, and we sails for that Santa Palma town on a line steamer. On the way me and Tim sees flying fish and plays seven-up with the captain and steward, and already begins to feel like the highball kings of the tropic of Capricorn.

'When we gets in five hours of the country that we was going to introduce to long drinks and short change the captain calls us over to the starboard binnacle and recollects a few things.

' "I forgot to tell you, boys," says he, "that Nicaragua slapped an import duty of forty-eight per cent *ad valorem* on all bottled goods last month. The President took a bottle of Cincinnati hair tonic by mistake for tabasco sauce, and he's getting even. Barrelled goods is free."

' "Sorry you didn't mention it sooner," says we. And we

bought two forty-two gallon casks from the captain, and opened every bottle we had and dumped the stuff all together in the casks. That forty-eight per cent would have ruined us; so we took the chances on making that $1,200 cocktail rather than throw the stuff away.

'Well, when we landed we tapped one of the barrels. The mixture was something heart-rending. It was the colour of a plate of Bowery pea soup, and it tasted like one of those coffee substitutes your aunt makes you take for the heart trouble you get by picking losers. We gave a nigger four fingers of it to try it, and he lay under a coconut tree three days beating the sand with his heels and refused to sign a testimonial.

'But the other barrel! Say, bartender, did you ever put on a straw hat with a yellow band around it and go up in a balloon with a pretty girl with $8,000,000 in your pocket all at the same time? That's what thirty drops of it would make you feel like. With two fingers of it inside you you would bury your face in your hands and cry because there wasn't anything more worthwhile around for you to lick than little Jim Jeffries. Yes, sir, the stuff in that second barrel was distilled elixir of battle money and high life. It was the colour of gold and as clear as glass, and it shone after dark like the sunshine was still in it. A thousand years from now you'll get a drink like that across the bar

'Well, we started up business with that one line of drinks, and it was enough. The piebald gentry of that country stuck to it like a hive of bees. If that barrel had lasted that country would have become the greatest on earth. When we opened up of mornings we had a line of Generals and Colonels and ex-Presidents and revolutionists a block long waiting to be served. We started in at fifty cents silver a drink. The last ten gallons went easy at five dollars a gulp. It was wonderful stuff.

It gave a man courage and ambition and nerve to do anything; at the same time he didn't care whether his money was tainted or fresh from the Ice Trust. When that barrel was half gone Nicaragua had repudiated the National Debt, removed the duty on cigarettes and was about to declare war on the United States and England.

' 'Twas by accident we discovered this king of drinks, and 'twill be by good luck if we strike it again. For ten months we've been trying. Small lots at a time, we've mixed barrels of all the harmful ingredients known to the profession of drinking. Ye could have stocked ten bars with the whiskies, brandies, cordials, bitters, gins and wines me and Tim have wasted. A glorious drink like that to be denied to the world! 'tis a sorrow and a loss of money. The United States as a nation would welcome a drink of the sort, and pay for it.'

All the while McQuirk had been carefully measuring and pouring together small quantities of various spirits, as Riley called them, from his latest pencilled prescription. The completed mixture was of a vile, mottled chocolate colour. McQuirk tasted it, and hurled it, with appropriate epithets, into the waste sink.

' 'Tis a strange story, even if true,' said Con. 'I'll be going now along to my supper.'

'Take a drink,' said Riley. 'We've all kinds except the lost blend.'

'I never drink,' said Con, 'anything stronger than water. I am just after meeting Miss Katherine by the stairs. She said a true word. "There's not anything," says she, "but is better off for a little water." '

When Con had left them Riley almost felled McQuirk by a blow on the back.

'Did ye hear that?' he shouted. 'Two fools are we. The six

dozen bottles of 'pollinaris we had on the ship – ye opened them yourself – which barrel did ye pour them in – which barrel, ye mud-head?'

'I mind,' said McQuirk, slowly, ''twas in the second barrel we opened. I mind the blue piece of paper pasted on the side of it.'

'We've got it now,' cried Riley. ''Twas that we lacked. 'Tis the water that does the trick. Everything else we had right. Hurry, man, and get two bottles of 'pollinaris from the bar, while I figure out the proportionments with me pencil.'

An hour later Con strolled down the sidewalk toward Kenealy's café. Thus faithful employees haunt, during their recreation hours, the vicinity where they labour, drawn by some mysterious attraction.

A police patrol wagon stood at the side door. Three able cops were half carrying, half hustling Riley and McQuirk up its rear steps. The eyes and faces of each bore the bruises and cuts of sanguinary and assiduous conflict. Yet they whooped with strange joy, and directed upon the police the feeble remnants of their pugnacious madness.

'Began fighting each other in the back room,' explained Kenealy to Con. 'And singing! That was worse. Smashed everything pretty much up. But they're good men. They'll pay for everything. Trying to invent some new kind of cock-tail, they was. I'll see they come out all right in the morning.'

Con sauntered into the back room to view the battlefield. As he went through the hall Katherine was just coming down the stairs.

'Good evening again, Mr Lantry,' said she. 'And is there no news from the weather yet?'

'Still threatens r-rain,' said Con, slipping past with red in his smooth, pale cheek.

Riley and McQuirk had indeed waged a great and friendly battle. Broken bottles and glasses were everywhere. The room was full of alcohol fumes; the floor was variegated with spirituous puddles.

On the table stood a thirty-two-ounce glass graduated measure. In the bottom of it were two tablespoonfuls of liquid – a bright golden liquid that seemed to hold the sunshine a prisoner in its auriferous depths.

Con smelled it. He tasted it. He drank it.

As he returned through the hall Katherine was just going up the stairs.

'No news yet, Mr Lantry?' she asked, with her teasing laugh.

Con lifted her clear from the floor and held her there.

'The news is,' he said, 'that we're to be married.'

'Put me down, sir!' she cried indignantly, 'or I will – Oh, Con, where, oh, wherever did you get the nerve to say it?'

One Thousand Dollars

'One thousand dollars,' repeated Lawyer Tolman solemnly and severely, 'and here is the money.'

Young Gillian gave a decidedly amused laugh as he fingered the thin package of new fifty-dollar notes.

'It's such a confoundedly awkward amount,' he explained, genially, to the lawyer. 'If it had been ten thousand a fellow might wind up with a lot of fireworks and do himself credit. Even fifty dollars would have been less trouble.'

'You heard the reading of your uncle's will,' continued Lawyer Tolman, professionally dry in his tones. 'I do not know if you paid much attention to its details. I must remind you of one. You are required to render to us an account of the manner of expenditure of this one thousand dollars as soon as you have disposed of it. The will stipulates that. I trust that you will so far comply with the late Mr Gillian's wishes.'

'You may depend upon it,' said the young man politely, 'in spite of the extra expense it will entail. I may have to engage a secretary. I was never good at accounts.'

Gillian went to his club. There he hunted out one whom he called Old Bryson.

Old Bryson was calm and forty and sequestered. He was in a corner reading a book, and when he saw Gillian approaching he sighed, laid down his book and took off his glasses.

'Old Bryson, wake up,' said Gillian. 'I've a funny story to tell you.'

'I wish you would tell it to someone in the billiard-room,'

said Old Bryson. 'You know how I hate your stories.'

'This is a better one than usual,' said Gillian, rolling a cigarette, 'and I'm glad to tell it to you. It's too sad and funny to go with the rattling of billiard balls. I've just come from my late uncle's firm of legal corsairs. He leaves me an even thousand dollars. Now, what can a man possibly do with a thousand dollars?'

'I thought,' said Old Bryson, showing as much interest as a bee shows in a vinegar cruet, 'that the late Septimus Gillian was worth something like half a million.'

'He was,' assented Gillian joyously, 'and that's where the joke comes in. He's left his whole cargo of doubloons to a microbe. That is, part of it goes to the man who invents a new bacillus, and the rest to establish a hospital for doing away with it again. There are one or two trifling bequests on the side. The butler and the housekeeper get a seal ring and ten dollars each. His nephew gets one thousand dollars.'

'You've always had plenty of money to spend,' observed Old Bryson.

'Tons,' said Gillian. 'Uncle was the fairy godmother as far as an allowance was concerned.'

'Any other heirs?' asked Old Bryson.

'None.' Gillian frowned at his cigarette and kicked the up-holstered leather of a divan uneasily. 'There is a Miss Hayden, a ward of my uncle who lived in his house. She's a quiet thing – musical – the daughter of somebody who was unlucky enough to be his friend. I forgot to say that she was in on the seal ring and ten-dollar joke, too. I wish I had been. Then I could have had two bottles of brut, tipped the waiter with the ring, and had the whole business off my hands. Don't be superior and insulting, Old Bryson – tell me what a fellow can do with a thousand dollars.'

Old Bryson rubbed his glasses and smiled. And when Old Bryson smiled, Gillian knew that he intended to be more offensive than ever.

'A thousand dollars,' he said, 'means much or little. One man may buy a happy home with it and laugh at Rockefeller. Another could send his wife South with it and save her life. A thousand dollars would buy pure milk for one hundred babies during June, July and August, and save fifty of their lives. You could count upon a half-hour's diversion with it at faro in one of the fortified art galleries. It would furnish an education to an ambitious boy. I am told that a genuine Corot was secured for that amount in an auction room yesterday. You could move to a New Hampshire town and live respectably two years on it. You could rent Madison Square Garden for one evening with it, and lecture your audience, if you should have one, on the precariousness of the profession of heir-presumptive.'

'People might like you, Old Bryson,' said Gillian, always unruffled, 'if you wouldn't moralise. I asked you to tell me what I could do with a thousand dollars.'

'You?' said Bryson, with a gentle laugh. 'Why, Bobby Gillian, there's only one logical thing you could do. You can go buy Miss Lotta Lauriere a diamond pendant with the money, and then take yourself off to Idaho and inflict your presence upon a ranch. I advise a sheep ranch, as I have a particular dislike for sheep.'

'Thanks,' said Gillian, rising, 'I thought I could depend upon you, Old Bryson. You've hit on the very scheme. I wanted to chuck the money in a lump, for I've got to turn in an account for it, and I hate itemising.'

Gillian phoned for a cab and said to the driver: 'The stage entrance of the Columbine Theatre.'

Miss Lotta Lauriere was assisting Nature with a powder puff, almost ready for her call at a crowded matinee, when her dresser mentioned the name of Mr Gillian.

'Let it in,' said Miss Lauriere. 'Now, what is it, Bobby? I'm going on in two minutes.'

'Rabbit-foot your right ear a little,' suggested Gillian critically. 'That's better. It won't take two minutes for me. What do you say to a little thing in the pendant line? I can stand three ciphers with a figure one in front of 'em.'

'Oh, just as you say,' carolled Miss Lauriere. 'My right glove, Adams. Say, Bobby, did you see that necklace Della Stacey had on the other night? Twenty-two hundred dollars it cost at Tiffany's. But of course – pull my sash a little to the left, Adams.'

'Miss Lauriere for the opening chorus!' cried the call-boy without.

Gillian strolled out to where his cab was waiting. 'What would you do with a thousand dollars if you had it?' he asked the driver.

'Open a s'loon,' said the cabby promptly and huskily. 'I know a place I could take money in with both hands. It's a four-story brick on a corner. I've got it figured out. Second story – Chinks and chop suey; third floor – manicures and foreign missions; fourth floor – pool room. If you was thinking of putting up the cap—'

'Oh, no,' said Gillian, 'I merely asked from curiosity. I take you by the hour. Drive till I tell you to stop.'

Eight blocks down Broadway Gillian poked up the trap with his cane and got out. A blind man sat upon a stool on the sidewalk selling pencils. Gillian went out and stood before him.

'Excuse me,' he said, 'but would you mind telling me what you would do if you had a thousand dollars?'

'You got out of that cab that just drove up, didn't you?' asked the blind man.

'I did,' said Gillian.

'I guess you are all right,' said the pencil dealer, 'to ride in a cab by daylight. Take a look at that, if you like.'

He drew a small book from his coat pocket and held it out. Gillian opened it, and saw that it was a bank deposit book. It showed a balance of $1,785 to the blind man's credit.

Gillian returned the book and got into the cab.

'I forgot something,' he said. 'You may drive to the law offices of Tolman & Sharp, at — Broadway.'

Lawyer Tolman looked at him hostilely and enquiringly through his gold-rimmed glasses.

'I beg your pardon,' said Gillian cheerfully, 'but may I ask you a question? It is not an impertinent one, I hope. Was Miss Hayden left anything by my uncle's will besides the ring and the ten dollars?'

'Nothing,' said Mr Tolman.

'I thank you very much, sir,' said Gillian, and out he went to his cab. He gave the driver the address of his late uncle's home.

Miss Hayden was writing letters in the library. She was small and slender and clothed in black. But you would have noticed her eyes. Gillian drifted in with his air of regarding the world as inconsequent.

'I've just come from old Tolman's,' he explained. 'They've been going over the papers down there They found a' – Gillian searched his memory for a legal term – 'they found an amendment or a postscript or something to the will. It seemed that the old boy loosened up a little on second thoughts and willed you a thousand dollars. I was driving up this way, and Tolman asked me to bring you the money. Here it is. You'd better count it to see if it's right.' Gillian laid the money beside her hand on the desk.

Miss Hayden turned white. 'Oh!' she said, and again 'Oh!'

Gillian half turned and looked out the window.

'I suppose, of course,' he said, in a low voice, 'that you know I love you.'

'I am sorry,' said Miss Hayden, taking up her money.

'There is no use?' asked Gillian, almost light-heartedly.

'I am sorry,' she said again.

'May I write a note?' asked Gillian, with a smile. He seated himself at the big library table. She supplied him with paper and pen, and then went back to her secretaire.

Gillian made out his account of his expenditure of the thousand dollars in these words: 'Paid by the black sheep, Robert Gillian, one thousand dollars on account of the eternal happiness, owed by Heaven to the best and dearest woman on earth.'

Gillian slipped his writing into an envelope, bowed, and went his way.

His cab stopped again at the offices of Tolman & Sharp.

'I have expended the thousand dollars,' he said, cheerily, to Tolman of the gold glasses, 'and I have come to render account of it as I agreed. There is quite a feeling of summer in the air – do you not think so, Mr Tolman?' He tossed a white envelope on the lawyer's table. 'You will find there a memorandum, sir, of the *modus operandi* of the vanishing of the dollars.'

Without touching the envelope, Mr Tolman went to a door and called his partner, Sharp. Together they explored the caverns of an immense safe. Forth they dragged as trophy of their search a big envelope sealed with wax. This they forcibly invaded, and wagged their venerable heads together over its contents. Then Tolman became spokesman.

'Mr Gillian,' he said formally, 'there was a codicil to your uncle's will. It was entrusted to us privately, with instructions that it be not opened until you had furnished us with a full account of your handling of the thousand-dollar bequest in the will. As you have fulfilled the conditions, my partner and I have read the codicil. I do not wish to encumber your understanding with its legal phraseology, but I will acquaint you with the spirit of its contents.

'In the event that your disposition of the thousand dollars demonstrates that you possess any of the qualifications that deserve reward, much benefit will accrue to you. Mr Sharp and I are named as the judges, and I assure you that we will do our duty strictly according to justice – with liberality. We are not at all unfavourably disposed toward you, Mr Gillian. But let us return to the letter of the codicil. If your disposal of the money in question has been prudent, wise or unselfish, it is in our power to hand you over bonds to the value of fifty thousand dollars, which have been placed in our hands for that purpose. But if – as our client, the late Mr Gillian, explicitly provides – you have used this money as you have used money in the past – I quote the late Mr Gillian – in reprehensible dissipation among disreputable associates – the fifty thousand dollars is to be paid to Miriam Hayden, ward of the late Mr Gillian, without delay. Now, Mr Gillian, Mr Sharp and I will examine your account in regard to the one thousand. You submit it in writing, I believe. I hope you will repose confidence in our decision.

Mr Tolman reached for the envelope. Gillian was a little the quicker in taking it up. He tore the account and its cover leisurely into strips and dropped them into his pocket.

'It's all right,' he said smilingly. 'There isn't a bit of need to bother you with this. I don't suppose you'd understand these itemised bets, anyway. I lost the thousand dollars on the races. Good day to you, gentlemen.'

Tolman & Sharp shook their heads mournfully at each other when Gillian left, for they heard him whistling gaily in the hallway as he waited for the elevator.